"I'm proposing we spend some time together," Steve suggested

"Neither one of us wants a romantic entanglement, and this is a sure way to avoid them. You and I… we'd both be on the same page," Steve added.

"Forgive me if I don't appear suitably impressed."

"See, I like that about you."

"What?" Chloe asked.

"That you speak your mind. That you're not easily impressed. We have a lot in common. Now, tell me what you do for fun."

Chloe was at a momentary loss. "I enjoy reading. And I do some knitting."

"And?"

"And…I don't know. I've been too busy to have fun."

"We can fix that." Steve's grin was a gradual progression from a smile, making it even more potent.

Dear Reader,

As the days get shorter and the approaching holidays bring a buzz to the crisp air, nothing quite equals the joy of reuniting with family and catching up on the year's events. This month's selections all deal with family matters, be it making one's own family, dealing with family members or doing one's family duty.

Desperate to save his family ranch, the hero in Elizabeth Harbison's *Taming of the Two* (#1790) enters into a bargain that could turn a pretend relationship into the real deal. This is the second title in the SHAKESPEARE IN LOVE trilogy. A die-hard bachelor gets a taste of what being a family man is like when he rescues a beautiful stranger and her adorable infant from a deadly blizzard, in Susan Meier's *Snowbound Baby* (#1791)—part of the author's BRYANT BABY BONANZA continuity. Carol Grace continues her FAIRY TALE BRIDES miniseries with *His Sleeping Beauty* (#1792) in which a woman sheltered by her overprotective parents gains the confidence to strike out on her own after her handsome—but cynical—neighbor catches her sleepwalking in his garden! Finally, in *The Marine and Me* (#1793), the next installment in Cathie Linz's MEN OF HONOR series, a soldier determined to outwit his matchmaking grandmother and avoid the marriage landmine gets bushwhacked by his supposedly dowdy neighbor.

Be sure to come back next month when Karen Rose Smith and Shirley Jump put their own spins on Shakespeare and the Dating Game, respectively!

Happy reading.

Ann Leslie Tuttle
Associate Senior Editor

Please address questions and book requests to:
Silhouette Reader Service
U.S.: 3010 Walden Ave., P.O. Box 1325, Buffalo, NY 14269
Canadian: P.O. Box 609, Fort Erie, Ont. L2A 5X3

The Marine and Me

CATHIE LINZ

MEN
OF
HONOR

SILHOUETTE **Romance**®

Published by Silhouette Books

America's Publisher of Contemporary Romance

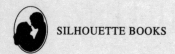 SILHOUETTE BOOKS

ISBN 0-373-19793-4

THE MARINE AND ME

Copyright © 2005 by Cathie L. Baumgardner

This edition published by arrangement with Harlequin Books S.A.

® and TM are trademarks of Harlequin Books S.A., used under license.
Trademarks indicated with ® are registered in the United States Patent
and Trademark Office, the Canadian Trade Marks Office and in other
countries.

Visit Silhouette Books at www.eHarlequin.com

Printed in U.S.A.

CATHIE LINZ

left her career in a university law library to become a *USA TODAY* bestselling author of contemporary romances. She is the recipient of the highly coveted Storyteller of the Year Award given by *Romantic Times* and has been nominated for a Love and Laughter Career Achievement Award for the delightful humor in her books.

Although Cathie loves to travel, she is always glad to get back home to her family, her various cats, her trusty computer and her hidden cache of Oreo cookies!

To all the wonderful librarians out there, like
Joyce Saricks, John Charles, Mary K. Chelton,
Lynne Welch and Shelley Mosley, among many others.
You all open so many doors to readers with your work
and dedication, and for that I thank you from the
bottom of my heart. Librarians Rock!

Chapter One

Steve Kozlowski had been in the Marine Corps for over a decade. He'd survived the most rigorous training in the world. He'd faced hostile forces in Afghanistan, survived temperatures of over one hundred and thirty degrees Fahrenheit wearing full-battle gear, seen the worst of conditions on half the continents on the planet.

He was one of the few, the proud, the tough.

Which meant he could handle his matchmaking Polish grandmother, no problem.

Even if his Busha was after him to meet the book-worm librarian next door, Steve could handle it. Or so he told himself. If necessary, he'd use evasive maneuvers to sidestep any matrimonial-minded booby traps that may have been laid down for his benefit.

That was the plan.

The reality was that he'd waited a minute too long.

The knock on the back door told him that much.

Steve could ignore it. He could sneak out the front door while his grandmother was in the bathroom.

But that smacked of cowardice, and Marines were not cowards.

"Aren't you going to open the door?" Wanda called out from down the hall, obviously hearing the continued knocking.

"Affirmative." Steve briskly yanked the kitchen door wide open.

A female stood there, frowning at him. "Uh, um, I'm looking for Wanda?"

"And you are?" As if he didn't know.

"I'm Chloe Johnson from next door."

"Right. Chloe the librarian. I should have guessed." He nodded at her dumpy clothes—the charcoal-gray sweater that looked two sizes too big, the white parochial-school shirt and black skirt that sagged around her ankles. The combat-style boots were a bit of a surprise, however.

Her dark hair was in a tight bun on top of her head. She wore black-rimmed glasses that stood out against her pale skin like ink on a newspaper. She had to be the mousiest woman he'd ever seen.

"My grandmother is unavailable at the moment." Steve deliberately kept his voice low, so as not to scare the poor female.

"Oh, uh…" She glanced around the room as if searching for something. "She told me to stop by and pick up some *kolachkis* for the library event tonight."

"Right." He'd already stolen three from the plate. "Here you go."

"Thanks."

"I'm Wanda's grandson, Steve, by the way."

She nodded. "Nice to meet you. Bye."

An instant later she was gone.

A minute after that, his grandmother reappeared in the kitchen and beamed at him. "So what did you think of Chloe? Isn't she a sweet girl? Better than those wild women you seem to favor."

Steve had to admit that in the past his taste in women had tended to lean toward good-time girls.

Then he'd met Gina. She'd been classy and smart.

He'd thought Gina was different. He'd been wrong. Thanks to an unexpected inheritance from his deceased Texas-oil-baron grandfather, Steve was a Marine with money. Lots of it.

That's what had interested Gina. The money. Not him.

The recent betrayal still cut deep.

Gina had conned him, saying she loved him when she really loved his bank account.

Humiliated by his own gullibility, Steve had come home on leave to the people he could trust—his family. He definitely wasn't looking to get into another romantic relationship. No way, no how. He'd visit his family for a while, then he planned on hitting the open road on his Harley, enjoying his freedom before returning to Camp Pendleton in California where he was stationed.

"Steve?" Wanda tugged on his arm to get his attention. "You haven't said, what did you think of Chloe?"

"She looked like a librarian."

Wanda frowned.

"She's not really my type," Steve added.

Wanda wagged her index finger at him. "You can't know that from one brief meeting."

Sure he could.

But he could tell by the stubborn tilt of her head that there was no convincing his Busha of that.

Wanda peered out through two of the aluminum blinds covering her kitchen window. "Oh, my. It looks like Chloe is having some kind of car trouble. You should go help her."

Sighing, Steve went outside to find Chloe leaning over the side of a compact car. The pose drew his attention to her bottom. Considering the fact that she was dressed like a nun, he felt guilty for even observing the fact that she had curves beneath those ugly clothes.

"What's the problem?" he gruffly asked.

"I don't know." Chloe straightened. "It won't start. And I've got to be at the library in fifteen minutes."

"Give her a lift," Wanda called out through the now-open back door.

Looking at Chloe's flushed face, Steve felt sorry for her.

"Take my car," Wanda added. "Not that motorbike of yours."

His Harley was not a mere motorbike, but he saw no point in arguing that fact at the moment.

So much for his battle plan. Busha had clearly won this first skirmish. But the war wasn't over with yet.

This wasn't the first time Wanda had tried to fix Chloe up, but it was definitely the worst. For the past few days, Chloe had heard all about Wanda's grandson Steve. She'd seen all the pictures of his good-looking face and lean body standing tall and proud in a U.S. Marines dress-blues uniform. She'd smiled politely as Wanda had confessed that Steve was something of a ladies' man, but that he was really only looking for the right woman, and then he'd settle down like his older married brothers.

Chloe wasn't buying that. She'd recently broken up with a ladies' man. She'd been blindly in love with Brad Teague, a handsome commodities broker. Her vision had been restored when she'd seen him kissing another woman and leading her up to his apartment.

Brad hadn't shown a bit of remorse as he'd informed her that it wasn't natural for a man to settle for just one woman.

She'd informed Brad that he could go jump into Lake Michigan.

Like Brad, Steve Kozlowski was good-looking, confident, sexy.

Like Brad, Steve judged a woman by her appearance. She'd seen the way Steve had looked at her when she'd walked into Wanda's kitchen. He'd dismissed her as someone not worthy of his attention.

Which was just the way she wanted it.

She hadn't anticipated the pity, however. That still stung. His expression as he'd helped her into his grandmother's car had been downright humiliating.

"Are you cold? Would you like me to turn on the heater?" Steve asked her.

"I'm fine, thank you." The evening was one of those perfect September examples of an autumn Chloe waited for all year. This was her favorite season—the crisp freshness to the air, the changing leaves, the toffee apples in the local market. Oh, yes, she was Fall's Number-One Fan.

"So, Chloe, what made you decide to become a librarian?"

His question was voiced with a politeness that she felt covered an underlying lack of interest in the answer. So she was brief. "I like books. What made you decide to become a Marine?"

"I like blowing up things."

She shot him a startled look.

He grinned at her. "Just checking to see if you were listening."

Oh, she'd been listening, all right. And looking. Despite the fact that she shouldn't. She shouldn't have noticed the way tiny laugh lines webbed out from the corners of his green eyes, or the way his light blue T-shirt clung to his wide shoulders, or the way his lower lip was full and surprisingly pleasing to look at. Actually, all of him was extremely pleasing to look at—from the top of his dark, short-cropped hair to the soles of his size-eleven feet.

She knew his shoe size because Wanda had told her, while showing her a photo album filled with pictures of Steve, from a baby crawling around to a young man riding a bicycle.

While Chloe thought that Wanda was a real sweetie, she had no desire to jump into another relationship any time soon. She liked her life the way it was—quiet and secure.

There was nothing quiet about Steve. Even his voice held a powerful resonance, his tone that of someone accustomed to delivering orders and having them instantly obeyed.

"You need to turn right at the next light," Chloe told him.

"I remember. I used to visit the branch library when I was a kid and would visit Busha."

"You lived in this neighborhood?"

"We lived all over. We moved around a lot because my father was in the Marines."

"That didn't bother you?"

"Moving? No. The military is like a big family. Even though we might be going to a new state for a new billet, people went out of their way to make us feel welcome."

Chloe wondered what that would be like, to be made to feel welcome. It wasn't anything she'd ever experienced when she'd been growing up. Not after her parents had died when she was eight.

"How about you?" he asked. "Did you grow up around here?"

"Not in this neighborhood, but in Chicago, yes."

"What about family?"

"I'm an only child. My parents died when I was young. I've got an aunt, but we're not close."

The only thing her aunt was close to was her chemistry lab and her experiments. Sometimes Chloe had a hard time believing that the emotionally stunted scientist could be related to Chloe's warm and loving mother Marie Johnson. Marie had been outgoing and full of life. Her older sister, Janis, had been remote and cold.

Janis. The name had a sharp edge that had suited the woman, whose angular face looked as if all the human kindness had been sucked out of it.

"That's got to be a rough deal, not having family," Steve said. "I know mine drive me nuts sometimes, but I can't imagine my life without them."

Sometimes Chloe did try and imagine what her life would have been like had her parents lived. But doing so only reopened old wounds. There was little point in doing that. She had to deal with the cards life had handed her.

"We turn left up here. The library is on the corner."

Steve nodded. "And looks just like it did the last time I was here."

"There's parking around the back. If you could just let me off at the staff entrance there, that would be great." She reached down for two heavy tote bags and then tried to balance the plate of *kolachkis*.

"Hold on a minute." Steve reached out to touch her arm, covered by the baggy sweater. "Where's the fire?"

"What?"

"Let me park and I'll help you carry that stuff in."

"There's no need for that...."

"Sure there is. I'm protecting my Busha's *kolachkis* from going splat in the parking lot before anyone can enjoy them."

He efficiently parked the huge boat of a car, and then came around to open the door for her. Chloe would have opened it herself but she was momentarily distracted by the way he walked—shoulders back, head held high. He radiated a powerful presence merely by putting one foot in front of the other.

"Here, let me take that." Steve reached out and his fingers brushed against hers as he took the plate of *kolachkis*.

His touch created lightning, flashing up her arm as heat permeated her entire body. She could feel the magic of it, and it was so powerful that the breath was momentarily snatched from her lungs.

No, no, this wasn't part of the plan. This wasn't supposed to be happening!

Unfortunately, telling herself that had absolutely no effect. Sexual awareness still hummed through her. A total zing-zing thing.

As if sensing her thoughts, Steve's eyes met hers in a searching look. While unable to read his exact thoughts, she saw no mirroring awareness there in his smoky green eyes. And why should she? Unless the man had a nun fetish, there was no way he'd notice her dressed the way she was.

That was the plan. And it was working all too well.

The librarian had great legs. Steve had seen a flash of them as she'd jumped out of his grandmother's car.

Her creamy calves had risen up from her combat boots, the curve of her knee a real attention grabber.

Or maybe he'd just been imagining things, because as he helped her with the door at the library's staff entrance, she sure didn't look like anything other than a...well, a librarian.

"Thanks again." She set the tote bags on the floor and reached for the *kolachkis*. "You don't have to stay. I can probably get someone to give me a ride home."

Her obvious eagerness to get rid of him perversely made him want to stick around for a while. So instead of leaving, he merely went back outside and walked around to the front of the building and entered it that way.

It had been a long time since he'd stepped foot in a public library, but he remembered how he and his twin brother Tom would check out the latest *Star Wars* paperback and then go home and devour it.

There had been a few changes in the place since then. More computers, more READ posters, more audiobooks.

But his main attention was captured by the sign advertising tonight's program—a special whodunit mystery night.

"Are you here for the program?" The question came from a guy wearing a silk robe over a pair of dark pants. "I'm playing the role of Lord Grimley and this outfit is supposed to be my smoking jacket. I don't know who thought of this idea of library staff

playing the parts of the characters and having the patrons try and figure out who the murderer is in this
drawing-room drama," he grumbled as he tugged on
the sleeve of his robe. "The program's this way, just
follow me."

The meeting room was already crowded, so Steve
took a seat in the back row and studied the flyer that he'd
been handed on his way in. Sure enough, Chloe's name
was on it. Chloe Johnson playing the part of Miss Abbington, loyal secretary to Lord Grimley.

Steve didn't really pay attention to the various clues
that were given as the drama began. Instead he remained
focused on Chloe. Her shoulders were hunched forward
as if she were trying to make herself as inconspicuous
as possible. She reminded him of a nervous rabbit as she
jabbed her glasses back in place when they slipped
down the bridge of her nose.

So what was it about her that intrigued him?

That was the mystery that engrossed him as he sat
there watching her.

He knew the exact moment she saw him, because she
faltered a moment while delivering the line, "But Lord
Grimley was the last one to see George alive."

Steve was surprised at the glare she shot him a moment later. There had certainly been nothing mousy
about that. It had carried the punch of a grenade launcher.

So what was going on here? Because something
sure was.

Chloe couldn't believe Steve had the nerve to spy on
her while she was doing the library program. She'd told
him he could leave, that he *should* leave. So why hadn't

he? He wasn't the kind of man who normally spent an evening at the local library, she was sure of that.

Steve was a man of action. A Marine accustomed to the adrenaline rush of battle. A man who loved speed. She'd driven with him, she knew. The guy rode a Harley, for heaven's sake.

He stood out like a wolf in a bevy of docile hens. Most of the rest of the audience was collecting Social Security, not combat pay.

A frown from Martin Pritchett, the branch manager playing the role of Lord Grimley, let her know that she'd just missed a cue.

Chloe quickly recovered and the rest of the drama went by without a hitch. The audience was asked to write down the name of who they suspected to be the murderer on a slip of paper, which was put into a box decorated with question-mark wrapping paper.

Chloe had organized a drawing for several door prizes, including books by bestselling mystery authors.

Martin had the honor of finally revealing the murderer. "The guilty party tonight was actually none other than…" He paused for dramatic effect. Martin enjoyed being the center of attention. "The loyal secretary Miss Abbington. Shame on you, Miss Abbington." He shook a finger at her as she hung her head in remorse.

The audience seemed to enjoy the event, applauding enthusiastically at its conclusion. Or maybe they were just happy about the hot tea and goodies that Martin had invited them to consume. Chloe noticed that Wanda's *kolachkis* disappeared quickly.

Steve noticed the same thing. "Busha's offering seems to be quite a hit."

"What are you doing here?"

"Watching you."

She didn't like that answer, not one bit. And the intensity of her reaction surprised her. After all, she'd spent years learning to suppress her emotions, to stay calm, to remain invisible and not make waves. So why was it that one sexy Marine seemed to have the power to change all that?

He was invading her turf—the library. One of the few places where she felt at home, where she felt in her element. Surrounded by books and information, all cataloged and shelved in an orderly manner.

"I also thought I could give you a ride back home after this," Steve added as he reached past her for a cookie.

Chloe badly wanted to refuse. But the person with whom she'd thought she could hitch a ride had actually carpooled with someone else this evening, someone who lived in the opposite direction from Chloe's house.

Beggars can't be choosers. How often had Janis told her that? Too often.

Steve polished off his cookie and reached for another. "My grandmother entrusted you to my care tonight. She'd shoot me if I didn't bring you back and make sure you got home safely."

So Steve was only doing this to please his grandmother? Somehow that didn't make her feel much better.

Chloe was glad when a patron interrupted them with a question about the name of a mystery author she couldn't remember. Helping unite people with books was what Chloe did best.

When the patron walked out with the book she'd wanted, Chloe was sidetracked by Lynn Scott, the children's librarian. "Who's the hottie you were talking to earlier?"

"He's my neighbor's grandson."

"You have all the luck. My neighbor's grandson is a holy terror, aged three."

"My car broke down so he gave me a lift tonight."

"Seeing him gave me quite a lift, too," Lynn noted with a grin. In her mid-thirties with long dark hair she usually wore in a braid, Lynn was one of those people who brightened the world with their presence. She and Chloe had hit it off from day one.

"Don't let your husband hear you saying that."

"There's no harm in just looking," Lynn noted.

Chloe tried telling herself that as Steve drove her home a short while later. No harm in just looking. The glow of the streetlights passed over his face, creating sharp angles and increasing his good looks.

She shifted her attention to his hands on the steering wheel. His fingers were long and lean. As he tapped out the beat of a Rod Stewart song with his index finger, she couldn't help wondering how it would feel to have him tapping out a sensual beat on her body.

He had the radio playing so they didn't have to talk much. She was glad. Her thoughts were much too messed up for her to make polite conversation.

She wondered what he was thinking. Was he eager to get rid of her? Was he wishing he were someplace else? With someone else?

Why should she care? If she were smart, and she was, she shouldn't have any interest in Steve's thoughts. Or his body. Or his lean hands.

She'd never been the sappy sort to get all hot and bothered over a man. Not until she'd met Brad. And that experience should certainly have cured her of any desire to repeat past mistakes.

But there was no ignoring her reaction when Steve had touched her hand earlier.

Chalk it up to hormones, or sexual chemistry, or nerves. Whatever she called it, she was not about to act on it.

Chances were that after tonight, Steve would go out of his way to avoid her. Her plan was working. She should be pleased, not all restless and edgy.

He pulled into the driveway and turned off the car before turning to face her. "So do you want to tell me what you're up to?"

His question caught her completely off guard. "Wha-at are you talking about?"

"I just have this feeling that you're up to something."

"You're mistaken."

"Maybe I am. Maybe not."

"Thanks for the ride. Good night." A second later, she'd hopped out of the car and raced into her house.

Steve watched her go, noting her haste. Not the actions of someone with nothing to hide. So what was the little librarian next door really up to?

He found out several hours later while making a midnight raid on the fridge and the leftover roast beef Busha had stored there. As he entered the dark kitchen, he noticed that the kitchen blinds were rolled up. Which allowed him free visual access to Chloe's kitchen window, only a few feet away, also with the blinds rolled up. Unlike him, she'd turned on the lights as she looked in her fridge, on the other side of her kitchen.

"Well, I'll be…." Steve swore under his breath.

The dowdy librarian had been transformed into a sexy woman, wearing a Bears' jersey that went mid-thigh, allowing him a generous view of a pair of gorgeous legs.

He'd been had!

Chapter Two

Steve blinked and looked again. Maybe he'd just imagined Chloe....

Nope, there she was. Her dark hair was down around her shoulders instead of tightly pinned up. The silky strands fell around her shoulders in sexy disarray.

And there was no mistaking her long shapely legs. Steve had excellent night vision and he could see just fine how great her body really was. This was no frumpy librarian!

She'd deliberately made him think she was a stereotypical dowdy bookworm. Why? What kind of con was she pulling here?

His internal lie-detector system went on high alert. Steve hated being deceived. Especially by a female. Chalk it up to his bad experience with Gina. The memory of how she'd hoodwinked him still made his gut clench.

Steve couldn't believe he'd been had by another female. He'd sworn not to be taken in again, yet here he was, in the dark about the girl next door. The supposedly sweet neighbor who had given him a hard time tonight with her superior intellectual attitude.

If she'd been trying to get his attention, she had it.

But that was just it. She *hadn't* tried to get his attention. It was almost as if she'd gone out of her way to make him overlook her.

The same question arose again. Why?

Steve was tempted to go over there and demand answers, but it was after midnight. Not exactly the time to go knocking on someone's door.

That was okay. Steve could wait. He'd done plenty of that in combat. Sometimes a mission required patient surveillance in order to get good intel.

Yes, sometimes waiting worked out just fine. It made the ultimate confrontation all the more satisfying.

Switching on the coffeemaker Saturday morning, Chloe's gaze lifted to the vintage hand-painted wooden sign she'd put over the sink. Home * Sweet * Home.

Chloe loved her brick bungalow. Not a day went by that she didn't thank the Realtor gods for her good fortune in finding it. The instant she'd spotted the For Sale sign planted in the scrubby lawn, she'd immediately called the number listed. Once inside, she'd been won over by the generous rooms and abundance of natural light. She'd envisioned the possibilities instead of being turned off by the negatives, like the dated kitchen in garish green and maroon.

Nothing, not the chipped molding, scarred hardwood floors or the other blemishes around the house had deterred her. Those were cosmetic things that could be corrected by someone with the ability to look beyond the dull surface to the sound heart beneath it all.

In the thirties, these homes were the dream houses of working-class Polish, Bohemian, German, Irish and Italian families. Now this one was Chloe's dream house.

Some might find the architecture unappealing. She'd heard plenty of people say that the bungalows in this neighborhood all looked the same.

Chloe found comfort in the dependability of that sameness. Because you knew what you were getting.

But what you did with it, ah…that's where the creativity came in.

Chloe had done plenty with her bungalow. Not as much as she'd like, but she'd made some inroads on her to-do list in the three years since she'd bought it. And she'd done her research with the help of the Historic Chicago Bungalow Initiative. Thousands and thousands of the one and one-half story residences had been built in a semicircle around the city, sometimes called the "Bungalow Belt."

Compact in size, well-crafted, efficiently laid out, the house had only needed a bit of rehabbing. Okay, maybe more than a bit. She'd replaced the cracked linoleum floor in the kitchen with black-and-white tile before moving on to the rest of the house, going from the back of the house toward the front, through the dining room and then the living room.

She hadn't done it alone. Lynn's husband was a handyman and he'd done a great job working on Chloe's house. She'd done a lot of the work herself as well, like stripping the avocado-green paint from the Arts and Crafts-style glass-fronted cabinets in the living room and restoring the natural wood.

Ditto for the built-in china cabinet in the dining room. The floral-patterned Staffordshire set she'd picked up at a garage sale for ten dollars looked perfectly at home on the cabinet shelves. She paused to straighten the large serving dish next to a delicate teacup and saucer.

Chloe loved order. No doubt that was a result of the emotionally chaotic circumstances of her childhood. Janis had made it clear to the eight-year-old Chloe that she wasn't to mess up anything—Janis's schedule, her austere condo, her plans.

That wasn't the kind of order that Chloe wanted. She liked the kind that was warm and welcoming, but had a place for everything. Because that kept things from getting out of control. And Chloe had learned early on not to rock the boat, to fly under the radar and not to get wild or out of control.

Thinking about wild naturally led her thoughts to Steve and her reaction to his simplest touch last night. Racing hearts were not in her plans. She'd taken a chance with Brad and look how that had ended up. Not good.

No, it didn't pay to depend on others for your happiness. A house was a much more reliable thing.

Her thoughts returned to her bungalow. The living room and dining room were completed but now she had to focus on the kitchen. She'd downloaded information from the Internet about proper restoration, replacing fixtures that didn't match the period or design of the house was a no-no. Someone at work had told her that one of the home-improvement stores had a big sale coming up, so Chloe was eager to check the sale flyers in her Saturday newspaper.

Chloe was thinking about kitchen faucets when she opened her front door to grab her newspaper, as she did every Saturday morning. In some places the newspaper was dropped at the sidewalk near the street, but here it was still delivered to the front porch.

Since she was only wearing her Chicago Bears nightshirt, she let the door provide cover for her while she leaned down to reach…nothing.

She reached farther…and touched warm flesh.

"Ahhh!" Startled, Chloe fell backward, ending up in a heap on her foyer floor.

"Hey, are you okay?" Steve inquired from above her.

She frantically tugged on the hem of her nightshirt, trying to cover what she could. "What are you doing here?"

"What are you doing down there?"

"Looking for dust bunnies," she retorted tartly before scrambling to her feet.

"Dust bunnies, huh?" He grinned at her. "Find any?"

She reached behind her for the afghan Wanda had crocheted for her last Christmas, yanking it from the reading chair and wrapping it around herself. "I did not invite you in," she pointed out.

"I wanted to make sure you're okay."

"I was until you grabbed my hand on the front porch."

Steve shrugged, drawing her attention to the broad shoulders beneath his dark pullover. "I thought you were reaching for me."

"I was reaching for my newspaper. I didn't know you were out there. What *were* you doing out there?"

"Like I said, I came to talk to you."

"About what?"

"About this disguise of yours."

She blinked at him and lifted her chin before tugging the afghan a little tighter around her shoulders, like

Queen Victoria gathering her royal robes. "I have no idea what you're talking about."

"Sure you do. I want to know why you were dressed the way you were last night."

"And what way might that be?"

"You know very well what way. Like a frumpy librarian."

"Isn't that what you were expecting?"

Steve hadn't expected her to turn the tables on him and put him on the spot. "It doesn't matter what I was expecting."

"Why not?"

"Because you're the one who was being deceitful."

"In what way?"

"By making me think you were…"

"Yes," she prompted him. "Go on."

He sensed dangerous foot-in-mouth quicksand ahead. "That you were something you're not."

"I can assure you, I *am* a librarian. You saw me at work last night."

"I also saw you raiding your fridge at midnight. And I'm seeing you right now."

"So?"

"So you don't look the same way you did when you came knocking on my grandmother's door last night. And I want to know why. Why the deception?"

"It wasn't a deception. I was merely wearing my costume for the library program last night. The whodunit mystery program, remember? You were there."

"Yes, I was there."

"Then what's the problem?"

"The problem is that I don't like being made a fool of." His voice reflected his irritation.

"If you feel that you acted foolishly, then you accomplished that all by yourself. You didn't need any help from me."

"What were you hoping to accomplish by dressing that way?"

"Why do you care?"

"Chalk it up to my natural curiosity. You're obviously an attractive woman. I can't help wondering why you tried to disguise that fact last night."

He thought she was attractive? Her ego soared before she shot it down with the reminder that this was a man accustomed to saying whatever a woman wanted to hear. She was smart enough not to fall for that. Right? She was also smart enough to get more clothes on ASAP. It was difficult to maintain one's dignity wrapped in an afghan. "I am not having this conversation half-dressed."

"You look fine to me."

She glared at him. "And you're the type of man to judge a woman by her appearance as to whether or not she's worthy of your attention, aren't you?"

"Am I?"

"You proved it by the way you reacted when I walked into Wanda's kitchen yesterday evening. You dismissed me."

"I had no idea they taught you to read minds in library school."

"It was obvious." She lifted her hand to her glasses, adjusting the frames before fixing him with a direct stare that dared him to fib.

"Okay, I admit I may not have been thrilled to see you," Steve admitted, "but it had nothing to do with you or how you looked."

"Right," Chloe scoffed.

"Look, I was just feeling a little…aggravated with my matchmaking grandmother for her heavy-handed attempts to hook me up with the girl next door."

"So you would have reacted the same way had a gorgeous lingerie model walked into your grandmother's kitchen?"

She had him there. And she knew it. He hated when that happened.

That didn't stop him from trying to defend himself. "I recognize your attack for what it is, an attempt to deflect attention from your own behavior."

"*I* behaved perfectly fine."

"By dressing up like a frumpy librarian?"

"I told you, I was wearing a costume—"

"You certainly were. And not just for that mystery thing last night. You didn't want me to know how good-looking you really are. Why?"

Instead of answering his question, she said, "I need more coffee. And I need to get dressed. Coffee first." She turned and headed for the kitchen.

"No need to do that on my account." If he were a better man, Steve would have told her that the afghan still left a tantalizing display of her bare thighs for his appreciation. Instead he noted the way she managed to walk all uptight and offended and still be sexy.

She removed an extra mug from the cabinet and reluctantly nudged it across the counter toward him. "I suppose you could drink a cup while I get dressed. Or you could go home…."

"No chance of that."

Chloe took her coffee mug filled with coffee into her bedroom with her, no easy feat given the fact that she was still holding the afghan around her body. Fifteen minutes later, the caffeine was finally hitting her system, giving her the energy to face the sexy but exasperating Marine in her kitchen.

She was dressed in a pair of tailored khakis and a white shirt, but she didn't like the way she looked in the mirror above her cherry dresser. So she changed and put on a T-shirt. A plain navy one. She'd quickly run a brush through her shoulder-length hair and decided not to take the time to do more with it. Who knew what Steve might be up to in her kitchen?

He was up to the sports section of her newspaper, calmly sitting at her kitchen table, looking as comfortable as if he'd been there every morning for the past year.

He glanced up and then gave her a slow smile. "So you're a Bears fan, huh?"

It took her a moment to realize that he was referring to the nightshirt she'd worn when he'd first arrived. That's because she was thrown by his smile and the effect it had on her. His smile was entirely too disarming. Wicked and tantalizing at the same time. Very much like the man himself, she suspected.

She had to remind herself that this was a man accustomed to seducing women. Not that Wanda had exactly put it like that, but she'd said how "popular Steve is with the ladies." Chloe could tell that much on her own. Steve possessed the same kind of inherent confidence that Brad had. And he was even better looking than Brad. Not a good mix.

"Shouldn't you be getting back to your grandmother's house?" she said.

"Not until I get some answers. You still haven't told me why you deliberately tried to deceive me."

"That's rather egotistical of you. Assuming that everything revolves around you. That my behavior was a result of you."

"Wasn't it?"

His directness rattled her. So did the ease with which he made himself at home in her domain. He should have looked like a bull in a china shop. But he didn't. He fit in.

No, stop that thought right there! Delete, delete, delete.

Maybe if she answered his question, he'd leave. "Look, suffice it to say that you're *not* the only one Wanda practices her matchmaking on."

"Meaning?"

"Your grandmother is a sweetie, but she's been raving about you for weeks. And when you suddenly decided to visit her during your leave, she was over the moon. She was also intent on my meeting you."

"And your objection to that was…?"

"As I said earlier, I know your type." She still stood, her hands gripping the back of the oak kitchen chair as if doing so would prevent her from something she might later regret. Grabbing him or tossing him out—she couldn't be sure.

"What type would that be?"

"A player. And having just been through a bad experience with a man who informs me that it isn't natural for a man to settle for just one woman, I wasn't interested in being played, okay?"

To her surprise, his expression turned serious. "Okay. I can understand that. I just came off a bad experience myself. Which is why I got so upset about you conning me."

"That's not the way I'd describe it."

"That's how I viewed it. You wore those clothes to keep me at bay."

"You're only interested in me now because you think I look prettier than I did last night." There, she'd said it.

"I tried to get to know you last night, but you weren't cooperating."

"You were just taking pity on the frumpy girl," Chloe retorted. "You didn't really mean it." This was a sore point for her. "I've already been dumped by a guy who I thought was interested in me, only to find that he was merely biding his time until a prettier woman came along."

"Ah, betrayal. That's something we have in common," Steve said. "Bad luck in the romance department."

She eyed him suspiciously. "I find it hard to believe that you've got bad luck that way."

"Believe it."

"That's not what your grandmother thinks. She never mentioned anything about bad luck."

"She doesn't know everything, although she'd like me to think she does."

The devil on her right shoulder warned her that Steve could be conning her, trying to gain her sympathy. "Your grandmother is a wise woman."

"And a stubborn one. She's not going to give up on getting us together, you know."

"That doesn't mean we have to do anything about it."

"Trust me, my grandmother has a way of wearing you down," Steve noted.

"And I suppose you have a plan to counter that?"

"Of course."

"First tell me about the woman who betrayed you." It was a test. She half expected him to toss off her request with some slick response. When he hesitated, she added, "I told you what went wrong with my relationship."

"Yeah, you were going with a jerk."

That stung, indicating that her judgment where men were concerned was faulty. Which might be true, but she sure didn't appreciate him pointing out that fact. "Don't you have someplace else you need to be right now?"

"No. You asked me a question, and I'm going to answer it. Want some more coffee?"

"I can get it myself."

"I'm sure you can."

"And I suppose you'd like me to pour you some more coffee while I'm at it?"

"If you do, I'll share these with you…." He held up a bag from a local bakery.

"Where did those come from?"

He read the side of the bag. "The Busy Bee Bakery."

"I meant how did they get here?"

"I brought them."

"When?"

"This morning."

"You're telling me you went to the bakery in the fifteen minutes I took to get dressed?"

"No."

She tried not to grit her teeth in frustration. "Are you always this exasperating?"

"No, I can be *much* worse."

"That's great to hear."

He held up the bag and waggled it. "So, do you want some or not?"

"What's in the bag?"

If he'd said a chocolate éclair, she could have resisted the temptation. But when he said, "Brownies," she knew she was a goner.

"Are you interested?" he said.

"An even trade. A refill on your coffee for a brownie."

"Works for me."

She loosened her grip on the chair and busied herself getting plates out of the kitchen cupboard before taking the coffeepot over to the table to refill his mug. "I still don't know how you got these here." She pointed to the bag of brownies.

"I carried them."

"When? And don't tell me this morning unless you're ready to suffer the consequences."

"I had them in my hand when I first arrived, but when you reached for me…"

"I was reaching for the paper!" she corrected him.

"I dropped them on your front porch." He peered inside the bag. "Luckily they didn't suffer from that little mishap."

"And you retrieved them from my porch while I was getting dressed?"

"That's right. Are you always this intent on solving mysteries?"

"I like things to be in order."

"Marines like order, too. See, that's something else we have in common."

Chloe wasn't so easily convinced. "Before you distracted me with decadent baked goods, you were going to tell me about this romantic bad luck you had."

Steve wasn't sure what to say, which wasn't unusual for him. Confiding had never been his thing. And telling her about Gina meant telling her about his inheritance.

Who was he kidding here? His grandmother had probably already told Chloe about the money.

Was that why Chloe had acted the way she had? Was this all an elaborate hoax to get his attention by pretending to avoid it?

He couldn't help being suspicious, given his recent track record where females were concerned.

Then his logical side reminded him that he had no intention of falling for Chloe. There was no danger of that. Sure he was a bit intrigued by her, but he was only here in Chicago for a short period of time during his leave.

Not telling her would mean he was afraid to. So he bit the bullet and started talking. Reluctantly. In his own way and in his own time. "Well, you've probably heard the sad story before—poor guy inherits money and a beautiful woman cons him into thinking she's in love with him when all she really wants is access to his bank account."

"Were you in love with her?"

Love. That four-letter word that had ended up sucker punching him without warning. "I thought I was."

"How do you know she was only interested in your money?"

"I don't tell many people about it. I'm assuming my grandmother told you, right?"

Chloe nodded before hurriedly assuring him, "Believe me, I'm not interested in your bank account."

"You'd hardly tell me you were, now would you?"

"True." She shifted uncomfortably before quickly returning the spotlight on him. "But getting back to your story."

He could tell she didn't like talking about herself. Something else they had in common.

"This girl—" Chloe was saying when Steve interrupted her.

"Her name was Gina. She was smart and classy. Gorgeous. A real knockout. And I discovered the truth when I found her with a good buddy of mine. I overheard them talking. He'd told her about the money. I'd told him, never thinking…" His jaw tightened. What an idiot he'd been. "Anyway, they both duped me."

"What did you do?"

"Walked in and told them the game was over. Gina tearfully tried to tell me that I'd misunderstood."

"Had you?"

Steve shook his head. "I saw the guilt in my buddy's face."

"So it was actually a double whammy. You were betrayed by both a gold-digging woman and by your buddy."

"At least he wasn't a Marine," Steve said. "He was a civilian."

"Oh, that explains it then," Chloe noted dryly. "Civilians aren't to be trusted."

"Hey, I spill my guts to you and you respond by mocking me?"

"You were reciting facts of what occurred. That's not the same as spilling guts."

"Like I'm ever gonna get all sappy about stuff," he scoffed.

"That would never happen, right?"

"I'm a Marine." His voice was brisk and powerful. "We don't do sappy."

"Right. You do tough and in control."

"Affirmative."

"Except where it comes to your grandmother?"

"Affirmative. But I do have a plan."

"Why am I not surprised by that…?" Chloe murmured before taking her last bite of brownie.

"The way to combat my grandmother's matchmaking moves is *not* to launch a counteroffensive. That would only make her dig in her heels more. Instead, we lull her into thinking she's winning the battle."

"And how do we do that?"

"Simple." He grinned at her again. "We move in together."

Chapter Three

"Wha-at?" Chloe almost choked on the coffee she'd just sipped. "Wha-at…" *Cough.* "Did…" *Cough, cough, cough.* "You…say?"

In the blink of an eye, Steve was around the table, patting her back. His hands were large and powerful enough to pound, but they were surprisingly gentle. And they felt surprisingly good. "You're entirely too easy to set off, you know," he chided her.

"So you were just kidding?"

"About moving in together? Yeah."

"I had no idea Marines were such jokesters," she noted tartly before standing and gathering the beige stoneware. The sharp clinks of the plates indicated her irritation.

"I wasn't kidding about the rest, though. About making my grandmother think she's winning the battle. All it requires on our part is spending some time together.

Because I'm telling you, she won't stop. If she doesn't succeed in hooking me up with you, she'll just set her sights on someone else."

"Better the devil you know than the one you don't?" Chloe asked, setting the dishes on the counter next to the sink.

Steve nodded. "So what do you think?"

"That you're out of your mind."

"By that I take it you have a few reservations about my plan?"

"A brilliant deduction. And an accurate one."

He appeared unfazed by her reaction. "That's understandable I suppose. Because you haven't thought the plan through."

"And you have?"

"Formulating successful mission plans is what I do."

"And here I was thinking Marines were fighting for home and country."

"We are. All over the world. But this mission is different."

"It certainly is. It involves your grandmother."

"I'm not proposing we lie to her."

"No?"

"No. We *really* would spend some time together. Neither one of us wants romantic entanglements, and this is a sure way to avoid them. You and I…we'd both be on the same page." His grin was a gradual progression from a smile, making it even more potent. "Hey, a book analogy. That should be one you'd appreciate."

"Yes, well, forgive me if I don't appear suitably impressed."

"See, I like that about you."

"What?"

"That you speak your mind. That you're not easily impressed. We have a lot in common. Tell me some more about yourself and you'll see what I mean."

"What's there to tell?" She efficiently placed the plates in the dishwasher before closing the door. "You already know that I work at the library."

"What do you do for fun?" Steve asked.

Chloe was at a momentary loss. Fun wasn't something she'd actually had a great deal of experience with. There wasn't time. She had things to do, goals to accomplish. She'd always kept her eye on the ball....

"Do you like watching football?" Steve asked her.

She blinked. "What?"

"That Bears nightshirt you were wearing so well."

"It was a grab-bag gift from the Christmas party at the library."

"Okay, so you're not a big football fan. What else?"

"I enjoy reading. And I do some knitting."

"And?"

"And...I don't know. I've been too busy to have fun."

"We can fix that."

"That's not necessary. I think it would be better if we simply tell Wanda that this isn't a good time for matchmaking, that neither one of us is interested in a romantic relationship right now. She'll honor that."

Steve just shook his head sadly. "You don't have much experience with stubborn Polish grandmothers, do you?"

"She's not my grandmother."

"Doesn't matter. She's mine. And she's got both of us in her matchmaking sights. I'm telling you, there's no convincing her."

"Maybe you just haven't said the right thing to her. I think we should try talking to her sensibly first."

Steve shook his head. "Big mistake."

"I think that what you're suggesting is a big mistake."

"Do you have a better idea?"

"She's *your* grandmother. It's not my problem."

"That's what you think. You'll see. Until then, I took a look at your car earlier this morning. You need a new battery. I can install it for you if you'd like."

She blinked at his sudden change of subject. Was he giving up that easily? That was a good thing, right? That meant she'd persuaded him with her logic. Good for her.

The news that she needed a new car battery was not good. It was definitely bad for her. Chloe hadn't budgeted for auto repairs this month. Librarians weren't in the profession for the money. Her paycheck would never be filed under "higher tax bracket."

"I've worked on cars and stuff since I was thirteen," Steve was assuring her. "I spent a summer in Texas with my mom's father who was totally aggravated with me for being more interested in engines than in the oil and gasoline that goes into them. I've always been good at it."

"At aggravating your grandfather?"

"Well, yeah, that too. I meant at working on engines, repairing things."

"Is that what you do in the Marine Corps?"

"No. I'm a captain in the Marine Corps. But getting back to your car, you can check with my grandmother if you need a reference."

"Thanks, but I'll have it repaired by a mechanic."

"It'll cost you. I could get it done in no time and you'd only be out the price of the battery itself."

She hesitated.

Steve continued, "You'll pay three times more if you

have your car towed to a repair place and have them install it."

"What would you want in return?" She'd learned the hard way that there were always strings attached to offers of help.

"Hey, it would be great if you'd agree to my plan regarding my grandmother, but I really don't want anything in return."

"Nothing?"

"Okay, feed me. That would work."

"I'm not as good a cook as your grandmother."

"Few people are."

"But I do make a mean grilled-cheese sandwich."

"Sounds great to me."

Chloe wasn't sure how it had happened, but somehow he'd managed to insert his way into her day. In no time at all he'd gone to an auto-parts store and returned with the battery.

Chloe sat on the middle step of her back porch and watched Steve work. She had a scarf to complete by Monday for a raffle at the library to support literacy.

But her knitting sat in a pile on her lap as her attention strayed from *knit one, purl two,* to the sight of Steve's denim-clad backside as he bent over her car.

One of the library's regular patrons, Mrs. Denallio, had a T-shirt that she'd picked up on a trip to Las Vegas. Girls Go Nuts for Cowboy Butts.

Chloe was no expert on cowboys, but this Marine certainly had a very nice…backside.

She felt naughty for even thinking such a thing. What was wrong with her? She'd certainly never ogled Brad's posterior. Yet here she was, unable to look away from Steve. His jeans fit him to perfection.

She could tell he kept his wallet in his right back pocket. The denim there was lighter. Not that his wallet was thick or bulging.

Bulging…oh jeez. Now her thoughts turned really naughty.

She blushed. This was ridiculous. She wasn't an adolescent making cow-eyes at some guy in study hall.

"Hand me that wrench, would you?"

The sound of Steve's deep voice made her jump guiltily, her knitting needles tumbling off her lap onto the steps with a clatter.

"Sure." Her own voice sounded as squeaky as a mouse. She came closer and looked at the metal toolbox open on the ground. Finding what she needed, she handed him the wrench he'd requested.

He didn't look up as he held out his free hand for her to give him the tool. Her fingers brushed his as she transferred the metal object from her grasp to his. A startling hum of awareness traveled up her arm at the simple touch. Not a good sign.

She gathered her tattered self-control. "How's it going?" Translation—how long are you going to be draped over my car looking like an Adonis and making me drool like an idiot?

"No problems."

Easy for him to say. She had plenty of problems, not the least of which was her reaction to him. You'd think that her experience with Brad would have short-circuited any possible response to a great-looking man, but no. Not in this case.

She tried looking over his shoulder, as if she knew what he was doing.

"There, that should do it." Steve stood so quickly he almost knocked her off her feet.

"Oops. Sorry about that." He caught her, his hands gripping her arms with strength and seduction. The seduction part came from the soothing brush of his thumbs over her bare skin. "I didn't see you standing there."

Right. That's the way she'd wanted it. To be invisible. That was in her comfort zone. This wasn't.

She stepped away and slid her glasses farther up the bridge of her nose. "I'll go make our sandwiches then. You can clean up in the bathroom. It's down the hall," she added as he followed her into the house.

"Yeah, I know. This floor plan is like my grandmother's." But where his grandmother had her knick-knacks all over the place, Chloe only had a few things. She did have lots of books, though. They were on every shelf, every tabletop. Even so, they didn't make the place look messy.

As he washed up, Steve considered his reaction to Chloe. A knitting librarian who read for fun. She needed someone to show her how to have a good time. Not sexually, he wasn't the kind of guy to seduce a woman and leave. He was only in town for a few weeks, after all.

It seemed so simple to him. Neither he nor Chloe were looking for any kind of romantic entanglements in their lives. So it made sense for them to join forces.

Now he just had to convince her of that. But the moment he walked into the kitchen, he could tell by her defensive posture that she was ready for him to pitch his plan. Well-versed in tactical maneuvers, Steve decided to do the unexpected, and not bring up his plan.

Instead he made simple conversation, telling her about his drive on his Harley from California, where he was based at Camp Pendleton, to Chicago. She was surprisingly easy to talk to. She asked intelligent questions and was a good listener. She also laughed in all the right places, which pleased him no end.

She really did have the most expressive face. Even though her black-framed glasses occasionally shielded her eyes, the emotions still shone through. So did their sparkling blue color.

She wasn't frumpy. She wasn't drop-dead gorgeous either. She was somewhere in between. And she wasn't obvious. There was real depth here. Not all surface flash.

And she could cook. The grilled-cheese sandwich was as good as she'd promised. He ate two. She'd also added big bowls of tomato soup, complete with those little fancy crackers floating in it.

He could see her relaxing as time went on, making him think this would be a good time to reintroduce his plan into the conversation.

"You see, I'm not so bad, right? So maybe now the idea of our joining forces doesn't seem such a bad one."

"I still think being up-front with your grandmother is the best way."

He could see her getting all prickly again, so he didn't push it. She had a stubborn streak, and the more he pushed her, the more likely it was that she'd just dig in her heels.

So he changed the subject again, and proved he knew his way around a kitchen by clearing the table and loading the dishwasher.

"You cooked, it's only fair that I clean up."

She eyed him suspiciously. "Thank you. Thank you also for fixing my car. I appreciate it." Her voice was very polite. "But it doesn't mean I think your idea of us joining forces is a good one," she felt compelled to warn him.

"I just haven't convinced you yet. I will."

Steve was gone before Chloe could contradict his outrageous claim.

His self-confidence really was amazing. Well maybe not, given how good-looking he was.

And, in addition to that, he was a Marine. They were hardly known to be shrinking violets.

Chloe wondered what it would be like to be so sure of yourself. She had no idea. She'd never felt that way.

Or maybe she had before her parents had died. If so, she had no memory of it.

She'd learned to be self-reliant, but it wasn't really the same as self-confident. Not by a long shot.

The bottom line here was that for some reason, Steve brought out a certain wildness in her and she wasn't sure how she felt about that. Not sure at all.

Chloe always did her grocery shopping on Saturday afternoon. Today was no exception. It didn't matter that her morning had started out with Steve on her front step. It didn't matter that they'd had lunch together after he'd finished repairing her car. She had a schedule and she stuck to it.

So it really, *really* didn't matter that he'd looked so sexy draped over her car that she couldn't get that image out of her mind and was even now totally distracted by the memory.

The crash of another cart into hers made her jump. "I'm so sorry," she automatically said before belatedly realizing who she'd just hit. Or had he rammed his cart into hers? "What are you doing here?"

Was no place safe from sexy Marines? Not even the produce department in her local supermarket?

"Me?" Steve reached out for the nearest piece of produce. "I'm just standing here squeezing squash. How about you?"

"What are you talking about? You don't squeeze squash."

"Sure I do. Look." He rotated the vegetable in his capable hands.

"That's an eggplant you're holding."

He shrugged. "Okay, so I admit I'm no expert when it comes to vegetables."

"A meat-and-potato man, are you?"

"Affirmative. And you're probably one of those fancy-salad women, right?"

She wanted to cover up the three bags of salad she'd tossed into her cart. "I'll leave you to your shopping then." She took off.

"Hey, wait up."

Oh, no. He was coming after her.

She needed time to recover. Where to hide?

Then it hit her. She turned left into aisle fourteen. The one with the feminine hygiene products.

Sure enough, he didn't follow her.

Good.

Okay then.

Chloe took a deep breath and practiced some of the meditation techniques a yoga instructor had given at a presentation at the library a few months ago. Close your eyes and think of a happy place.

She thought of her bungalow. All completed. Everything perfectly done. Everything in place. Everything in order.

Yessssss. That was calming. She opened her eyes, a new woman.

A new woman…who turned the corner into the next aisle and bumped into Steve's cart again.

"What do you think? Barbecue or vinegar potato chips?" He held up the two bags for her perusal.

Okay, now she was getting aggravated. "Why are you following me?"

"Me?" He raised an eyebrow. "Why are *you* following *me?* I was here in the snack aisle first."

"I'm here to get things for Wanda."

"Me, too."

"What are you talking about?"

"She gave me a list."

"But she gave me a list, too."

"I'll show you mine if you show me yours." His voice went all low and sexy all of a sudden, making her think of rumpled black satin sheets and how he'd look spread out on them.

How could he have this kind of effect on her in the middle of a brightly lit supermarket? How was that possible? Was she coming down with something? Did she have a fever? Is that why she felt so hot all of a sudden?

The gleam in his green eyes told her that he knew he'd gotten to her. That immediately stiffened her resolve. "Here." She waved the list at him. "Where's yours?"

"Right here." He held it out for her inspection.

Chloe frowned. The lists were the same. "I don't understand. I called to tell her I was on the way to the store, as I always do, and asked if she needed anything."

"Bingo."

"What do you mean? She knew I was getting the things she needed. Why did she send you?"

"To bump into you. She told me I had to hightail it to this grocery store immediately. I did try to warn you that she'd be ruthless about her matchmaking."

"I hardly call this ruthless."

"Just wait, it'll get much worse."

"Has she done this to you before?"

"She's tried to. Normally I'm not around long enough or if I am, I'm able to talk my way out of it."

"Then do that now."

"I can't. She's wise to my moves."

"I find that hard to believe."

"It's true."

"Then come up with new moves."

"I don't want to spend my entire leave trying to dodge her. I'm telling you, it would be much simpler to just make her think she's succeeded."

"Simpler for whom? You maybe. I don't see the advantage to me."

"I have one thing to say to you. Roland Knab. You know who he is?"

Chloe nodded. "He runs an accounting business out of his home. He lives with his mother across the street from us."

"He's next in line."

"In line?" she repeated with a frown.

"As a candidate to be the man in your life."

"He's got to be fifty and he's almost bald."

"But he has a great personality, right?"

"Wrong."

"Too bad."

"What makes you think your grandmother would try and pair me with Mr. Knab?"

"Insider intel."

Chloe couldn't help wondering why on earth Wanda would think that Chloe had anything in common with the accountant. Was it because they were both the introverted type? Unless Steve was trying to con her? "Why should I believe you?" she asked suspiciously.

"Because I'm telling the truth. On my honor as a Marine." He solemnly placed his right hand over his heart. Of course that just drew her attention to his dark pullover and the breadth of his shoulders.

"Well, we'll just see about that." With those brilliant words, she took off, heading for the checkout line posthaste.

"Thank you so much for picking up these things for me at the grocery store," Wanda told her as she ushered Chloe into her kitchen a few minutes later. "Sit. I have some cookies just out of the oven."

Chloe wasn't sure where Steve was. She'd lost him in the crowd at the checkout line. "Umm, is your grandson around?"

"Not at the moment, no. You like him though, yes?"

She wasn't sure how to answer that one. If she were a bolder person she'd just confront Wanda and ask why she'd sent them both out for the same groceries.

But Chloe wasn't into confrontation. That made waves and she'd spent too many years avoiding them.

So she just made some noncommittal murmur and took a bite of the cookie.

Wanda didn't look all that imposing a figure. She was petite but a powerhouse. Her vivid light blue eyes had a way of looking at you and ferreting out your deepest secrets. She was warm, compassionate and caring. But she was also gazing at Chloe with clear expectation of an agreement on Chloe's part that Steve was the best thing since sliced bread.

Chloe needed a distraction. "Um, is that a new addition to your turtle collection?" She pointed to the ceramic figure on the kitchen table.

"Yes, it is. My grandson Striker sent it to me from Texas. It's a Texas turtle. See the little Stetson on its head?"

Chloe nodded.

Wanda had turtles all over the house. Dozens of them filled the shelves of the display cabinet in the living room. Ceramic, glass, silver, it didn't matter. She collected them all.

"Have I told you why I like turtles so much?"

Chloe shook her head, glad for the reprieve from a conversation about Steve.

"Because it carries its home on its back. If the turtle wants to move, it has to stick its head out. That means it has to take a chance. Otherwise it doesn't go anywhere."

Chloe wasn't sure if there was a message hidden in there someplace.

"My parents took a chance and got me out of Poland during World War II. I took a chance and married an American G.I. after the war, having only known him for two weeks. And he brought me to America." Wanda ran her hand over the ceramic figure. "The turtles remind me of the good that can come from taking chances. And from keeping your home with you, within you, so it goes where you go. All you have to do is stick your head out and look at the possibilities."

"By possibilities do you mean going out with your grandson?"

Wanda's expression brightened. "He's very good-looking, yes?"

"Yes. But honestly, Wanda, I'm really not looking for any kind of romantic relationship at the moment."

"So like the turtle you keep your head tucked in and move no place." Wanda clucked her tongue and shook her head. "This is not good." She reached across the table to pat Chloe's arm with concern.

"Sure it is." Chloe put as much reassurance as she could into her smile. "It's good for me right now. It's what I need."

Wanda didn't agree. "You need someone to love you. But if you don't like my grandson, I have someone else in mind for you. Roland from across the street is a turtle like you, not wanting to move. Two turtles might be good for each other." Wanda paused a moment to consider. "Yes, the more I think of it, the better that could be."

Chloe spent the next fifteen minutes trying to convince Wanda to leave well enough alone, that she didn't need a man in her life. To no avail. She was unable to make one iota of change in Wanda's thinking.

Chloe had just made her escape from Wanda's matchmaking clutches when Steve pulled up in Wanda's car. He stood there watching her as Chloe joined him.

"Tell me your plan again." She hoped her voice didn't sound as desperate as she felt.

Had his smile held one bit of I-told-you-so, she'd have willingly kicked him. Instead his grin was quick, reflecting pure masculine pleasure. "I'd be happy to. We can discuss it tonight over dinner."

Chapter Four

"Who am I kidding?" Chloe tossed another gray skirt onto the pile already gathered on her bed. "Nothing I wear is going to make a difference. It's not going to change me into something I'm not."

"Okay, that kind of talk is just untrue," her friend and co-worker Lynn declared, having joined Chloe after an agitated phone call for help. "Clothes are a costume. Look at what you wore to the mystery night. That wasn't you."

"I'm afraid it might be," Chloe noted glumly. How had her wardrobe gotten so blah? When had that happened?

Lynn placed a supportive arm around Chloe's shoulders. "Listen, if you can handle the reference desk at a branch of the Chicago Public Library, you can handle this with one hand tied behind your back."

"Maybe I'd look better that way."

"You're making a stand for librarians everywhere.

This is a chance to break all those stereotypes of us as mousy bookworms."

"I *am* a bookworm."

"Yes, but we can turn you into a well-dressed one. What about this black outfit?"

"I wore it to my former boss's funeral four years ago."

The dress joined the pile on Chloe's bed. Lynn continued her search. "Okay, how about red? Do you have anything red? It's a power color and with your dark hair and creamy skin it would look great on you."

Lynn efficiently moved through Chloe's closet until she found what she was looking for. "Ah, this is good."

"I've never worn it."

"I deduced that much from the tag still hanging on it."

"Maybe I should cancel. I hate this ritual, getting all dressed up to please someone else."

"Well, there's your first mistake. You're getting dressed up to please yourself. And me, of course. Here, go try this on in the bathroom."

Chloe did as she was told. She always did as she was told.

An unexpected wave of rebellion rose up within her. That's why she left the top two buttons of the red knit top undone.

Big deal, she mocked herself in the mirror.

Narrowing her eyes, she undid another button, as if daring her reflection to make fun of her now. Then another button was undone. Take that!

Wait, now her bra was visible. She quickly did up that last button.

Coward.

Since when had her reflection gotten so mean? "Listen, I don't need you insulting me," she sternly muttered to herself. "I've got enough on my plate as it is."

Wanting to get away from the mirror, she yanked open the bathroom door to find Lynn standing on the other side.

"Oh, yes." Lynn nodded. "That's looking good. Just needs a little tweaking. Undo another button and replace those black tights with these." She shoved an unopened package of black stockings at her.

Chloe was amazed at the difference the stockings made. They made her black skirt look much shorter than it had with the tights.

"Shoes," Lynn muttered. "We need shoes."

A few moments later, Chloe eyed Lynn's selection doubtfully. "Isn't it a little late to be wearing sandals? It's almost October."

"They look better than your combat boots or the Mary-Jane flats. At least these have a heel. Okay, now you need jewelry. Something to fit into that curve of your throat. A choker."

Lynn ended up using a piece of black ribbon and slipping a silver and black heart onto it. "You're good," Chloe noted with a nod of approval. "I should have you dress me more often."

"Here, borrow these marcasite drop earrings. I've never worn them. Okay, now some makeup. I'm telling you, it's a good thing my sister is a hairstylist and makeup artist or I wouldn't have a clue what to do."

"Like me." Chloe tried not to let her self-doubts overcome her again.

"You always look fine at work. But you're going for something else now."

"Yeah, and that something else is stupidity. What

made me think I could do this? You know how things ended with Brad."

"You're not going out with Brad."

"With someone very much like him."

"All good-looking guys aren't jerks."

"Just most of them."

"You know Steve's grandmother," Lynn pointed out.

"She's the reason I'm having to go through all this."

"I meant that knowing his grandmother means that chances are he's not going to mess up big time. You're just going out for dinner. No big deal."

"If it's no big deal, then why did I call you in a panic? And why did we just spend the past hour getting me ready?"

"So you'd feel confident."

"I think we're just going to the local Chinese place. I don't want to look too dressed up."

"You look fine."

Chloe nervously tucked a strand of her hair between her fingers. "Maybe I should pin my hair back or something."

"It looks nice loose like that."

"But the drop earrings keep getting stuck in my hair."

"Oh." Lynn reached into the small box on the dresser where Chloe kept her hair clips. "In that case, just use one of these to just fasten your hair up and away from your face. There, you're done."

"I'm done all right," Chloe muttered, wondering when the confidence would start kicking in.

"And stop buttoning up that button." Lynn slapped Chloe's hand away.

"You can see my bra."

"Not all the time. And it's a nice black bra, nothing to be ashamed of."

"Right. Easy for you to say. You're not going out with a Marine tonight."

"Believe me, I'd change places with you if I could, but I don't think my husband would understand."

"You know you wouldn't trade Dave in for anyone else."

"True." Lynn put her arm around Chloe's shoulders for a quick hug. "Just relax and enjoy your evening out. I'll get out of your way now. But call me as soon as you get home. I want to hear all about it."

Chloe felt a bit guilty for not telling Lynn about Steve's suggestion that they hang out together. But she didn't know how to explain things. And it wasn't as if Chloe had agreed to Steve's plan yet. She just wanted more information so she could make an informed decision. And so she could avoid Wanda trying to hook her up with Roland across the street.

To calm herself while waiting for Steve, Chloe picked a book out of her tote bag and started reading. As was always the case when she had a great book in hand, she was drawn into that world and it took her a moment to realize that Steve was at her front door. Using her bookmark to mark her page, she set the novel aside and hurried to the foyer.

Taking a deep breath, she checked her appearance in the mirror. Great, one side of her hair was sliding down. She quickly redid the clip and then opened the door.

"You okay?"

"Why?" She looked down at her top to see if her bra was showing. "What's wrong?"

"Nothing. You look great."

"Then why did you ask if I was okay?"

"Because it took you a while to answer the door. I

wondered if you'd gotten cold feet and changed your mind about going out tonight."

"Absolutely not," she fibbed. "Let's go."

Steve was once again driving Wanda's car. He opened the passenger door for her and held it open while she got inside. Then he closed it for her. His manners were impeccable. That wasn't something you saw much these days. Brad had rarely opened a door for her. She'd thought it was because he considered her to be a modern liberated woman. Now she wondered if he was just lazy and self-centered.

"I don't know how familiar you are with the restaurants in this area," Chloe began.

"Not very," Steve admitted.

"There's a nice Chinese place about a mile away. I often get takeout from there on my way home from the library."

She gave him directions but instead of following them, he made two right turns.

"Where are we going? This is the entrance ramp to the expressway," Chloe said.

"We're going to dinner."

"I thought we were going to the Chinese place."

"Nope."

"Then where are we going?"

"To a place in Lincoln Park. I think you'll like it."

Chloe *loved* it. The Arts and Crafts decor was near and dear to her heart. In fact, she wanted to take the light fixtures home with her.

They were led to an enclosed patio area where nine-foot glass French doors offered views of Lincoln Park on three sides. In the background was the Chicago skyline, the buildings rising up in sharp contrast to the natural fall foliage of the surrounding trees. No matter how many times Chloe saw that skyline, she was always amazed by it. A large fieldstone fireplace lent warmth and intimacy to the room.

She almost gulped when she saw the prices on the menu.

Reading her expression, Steve reminded her, "I'm a Marine with money."

"You won't be a Marine with money if you eat at places like this all the time."

"Don't worry about it. And if you try that dainty girl trick of just ordering a small salad instead of a real meal I'll be forced to order for you and you might not like what you get then."

"I don't like being ordered around."

"No, I don't suppose you do. You're probably used to being the one giving orders like 'Shhh!' and 'Put that book back on the reference shelf.'"

"Okay, just for that, I'm ordering the most expensive thing on the menu," she retorted.

She didn't, but it was only after their server had taken their order that she realized that Steve had deliberately pushed her buttons. He appeared to enjoy goading her. "You did that on purpose," she accused him.

"Did what?"

"Don't give me that innocent look. You can't carry it off anyway."

"I have no idea what you're talking about."

"I'm talking about how you used the stereotype of librarians to get me aggravated."

"You? Aggravated? No. Surely not."

She had to laugh at his mocking disbelief. "I admit I can be a tad stubborn sometimes."

"Same here."

They paused as their first course arrived. They'd both chosen the corn-on-the-cob soup. At her first mouthful, Chloe closed her eyes and *mmmm*ed with pleasure.

The expression of sublime pleasure on her face made Steve hot. She totally revved his engine. And she wasn't even trying. Was she?

He studied her closer. As an officer, he'd learned to read people. Not that he'd done real well in that department where Gina was concerned. She'd blindsided him. He wasn't about to be caught unprepared again.

Chloe appeared oblivious to his attention, which made watching her easier. Okay, that was a lie. When her tongue darted out to lick the soup from her bottom lip, his entire body tightened. He reached for some ice water, sipping it when he should have dumped it on his lap to cool down.

She suddenly looked up at him, her blue eyes meeting his with unabashed directness. "Is this awesome or what?"

"Awesome." How did this librarian manage to generate this kind of a reaction from him? Had he been too long without a woman, was that it?

"You're not eating yours," Chloe noted in concern. "Is there something wrong?"

Affirmative. Something was definitely wrong here. Off kilter. He was supposed to hang around with the girl next door, not lust after her.

"The soup is fine," he belatedly replied.

Things didn't improve with the arrival of their main course. He'd ordered the wild salmon and she had the sea scallops with toasted walnuts. Every time she placed a plump bite of the seafood into her mouth, he was engrossed with her enjoyment…and with her lush lips.

Why hadn't he noticed them before? Or had he? He was so muddled, he couldn't think clearly.

He'd told her earlier that she looked great and he'd meant it. She looked good in red compared to the non-descript colors she usually seemed to favor. Her sensual satisfaction with the gourmet food made him wonder if she'd be equally expressive in bed.

Whoa. *About face!* he ordered his thoughts. Do not go there.

What was he afraid of here? That he'd fall for the librarian? Come on. He was only in town for a few weeks. Besides, she wasn't his type.

Was he afraid that she was setting him up? Not a problem if he didn't fall for her.

He was just getting paranoid, that's all. This was a simple matter. Hang out with the devil you knew. Let his grandmother think he and Chloe were getting to know one another. Have some fun in the process. Leave. What was so complicated about that?

"You've been awfully quiet."

"Sorry about that." Steve felt much better now that he had his thoughts in order once more. "So how do you like this place?"

"I love it! Do you think they'd notice if I took one of these light fixtures home with me?" She pointed to the high ceiling.

"Yes, I think they would. And I don't think it would fit in your purse, so removing it from the premises might be difficult."

"That's what I was afraid of."

"What else are you afraid of?"

"Overdue books," she solemnly informed him. "The very thought keeps me up nights."

The librarian had a sense of humor. And great legs. Two things he liked in a woman.

They finished their meal with a bittersweet chocolate mousse accompanied by a hazelnut cookie wafer.

Chloe dabbed the last bit of chocolate from her lips with the linen napkin before proclaiming, "That was a meal to die for. But you still haven't told me about your plan."

"Right." Pay attention to the plan, meathead. Don't get distracted by luscious lips and darting tongues. He was a Marine, a breed apart. He had incredible willpower. He'd successfully completed the Marine Officer Candidates School, a physical, intellectual and emotional testing ground so grueling that every fourth candidate failed.

"As I said earlier, it makes sense for us to join forces to stave off Wanda's matchmaking ways. We both know the score. Neither one of us is looking for romantic entanglements. My grandmother is quite capable of trying to hook us up with other people, which would be much more problematic. But if you and I temporarily hook up, then we avoid that problem."

"I don't know what she could think I have in common with Roland. I've gotten into a rut, that must be it. Doing the same-old, same-old day after day. I used to like the reliability of that, but now I'm not so sure. I'm bordering on becoming staid like Roland," she muttered with displeasure.

"I can help you with that. Don't give me that look, I'm not talking about sex."

Her heart gave a funny leap at the sound of him saying that word. *Sex.* She prayed she wasn't blushing. That would make her staid *and* a prude.

"Then what are you talking about?" she asked.

"We join forces for a training mission. We'd work as a team. The Marine Corps is big on using the buddy system. The ability to work together to accomplish goals is crucial to the successful outcome of any mission."

"What kind of training mission?"

"Your goal is to lead a more adventurous life. I can help prepare you for that."

Her pride was stinging at the thought that she had to be *shown* how to have fun. How pitiful was that? Before she could say anything, Steve started talking again.

"It's the least I can do to try and repay you by helping me out. I'd still be deeply in your debt, but at least this wouldn't make me feel so badly about requesting your help."

Well, that made her feel better. A lot better. He needed *her* help.

"Look on it as a sort of adventure boot camp," he suggested.

Boot camp? That sounded a little excessive. "I'm not into extreme stuff like bungee jumping."

"That's not what I'm talking about. I'm talking about being spontaneous. That's something I'm real good at. That's how I got into trouble with Gina. I didn't know her all that long when I stupidly fell for her."

"If my goal is to lead a more adventurous life, then what's your goal?" Chloe countered.

"To be more cautious where personal relationships are concerned."

"I wouldn't call what you're proposing as being cautious. We haven't even known each other more than a few days and here you are suggesting we join forces and become a team."

"Right. A *team*. Not a couple."

Chloe paused. He had a good point. There was definitely a difference between the two. A rather large difference in fact. Teams worked together toward a common goal, but without the romantic elements of being a couple.

And yes, their goals were different, but they could help one another. What harm could come of it? She was tired of always overthinking everything.

"Okay. You've got a deal."

"Great."

"It will be a training mission for both of us."

"Affirmative."

"So does our team have a name? Like Alpha or Bravo or Charlie?" She was really getting into this now.

"How about Libras?"

"How about Alpha Libras?"

"Works for me."

"Me, too."

"Outstanding. Then allow me to propose a toast." Steve lifted his wineglass. "To Alpha Libras and the successful completion of our joint mission."

"Ooohraaaaaah! Did I get that right?"

He grinned. "Close enough."

As she clinked her wineglass with his, she reminded herself that she would not be getting close enough to Steve to fall for him. Instead she'd stick to the mission and emerge a new woman.

"So when's the wedding?" Steve's brother Rad demanded in a phone call very early Sunday morning. Rad was assigned to Camp Lejeune in North Carolina and had gotten married six months ago.

Well aware of the Kozlowski brothers' duty to drive

one another crazy, Steve was not thrown by Rad's mocking comment. "There's no wedding. Not gonna be one, so don't go holding your breath."

"I'm telling you, you've got to watch out for these bookworms," Rad warned him. "They've got a way of sneaking up on you, and wham, you're in over your head."

"Since when does a bookworm beat out a Kozlowski Marine?"

"Ah, spoken like a man who believes, mistakenly, that he holds the upper hand."

"I do hold the upper hand. I have a plan."

Rad groaned. "Yeah, I had a plan, too."

"I'm not talking about marriage."

"I hear you, bro. Marriage wasn't in my original game plan either. My original plan was to have Serena only pretend to be my fiancée."

"I didn't know that."

"That's why I'm telling you now, you're in for trouble."

"So you're having regrets you married Serena?"

"No way! Best move I ever made."

"Hey, I'm glad for you. But your experience has nothing to do with me."

"Yeah, well you and I might not be as tight as you and your twin are, but I'm telling you, there's more to these bookworms than meets the eye."

"Yeah, I've already discovered that much," Steve noted, remembering his heated reaction to Chloe last night.

"I rest my case."

"Fine, I'll be on high alert, and won't let my guard down."

"You do that and you won't have much fun."

"Since when have you become the fun brother?" Steve demanded. "I thought that was Tom's job."

"Hey, Serena told me she was attracted to that wicked gleam of humor in my brooding eyes."

"Was she drunk at the time?"

"Very funny."

"I'm certainly more humorous than you'll ever be."

"Who are you talking to?" Wanda demanded, having entered the kitchen in time to hear his last comment.

"Your dumbest grandson. Rad."

Wanda clucked her tongue at Steve even as she took the phone he handed her. "Ah, Rad, it is good to talk to you. Yes, I am fine. No, Steve isn't giving me too much trouble. I'm glad to have him here for a visit. He's met the nicest girl, did he tell you? No? You men never talk about the important things. How is Serena doing? Any more book signings with Sexual Goddess, Amelia Smith? No? That's too bad. Maybe you should have Serena ship a copy of that book up here for your brother."

Steve couldn't believe what he was hearing.

"Fine, thank you Rad. I love you. Give Serena a hug from me."

"What was that all about?" Steve demanded.

"Ah, were you jealous? I love you, too." She patted his cheek fondly.

"I wasn't talking about that."

"Then what?"

"You telling Rad to send me a book written by some sexual goddess."

"The author is much too old for you."

"I'm not interested in the author. I'm interested in knowing why you'd think I'd need such a book."

"I have read it, it's good."

Steve didn't even want to think about traveling down that road of discussion.

"Ah, look at your face. Rad looked just as stunned when I told him. You two." Wanda laughed and shook her head. For such a small woman, she had a huge laugh that filled the kitchen. "You'd think I knew nothing about sex."

"This is all Rad's fault," Steve growled.

"My knowing about sex?" Wanda laughed again. "No, I knew about it way before any of you were born. Before your father was born. But it is always interesting to pick up additional information by reading, don't you think?"

Steve didn't know what to think, let alone what to say.

Wanda then added, "Chloe loves to read, you know."

Was Chloe reading those kinds of books as well? Sex manuals? Suddenly the concept of her reading for fun got an entirely new twist.

"You should see your face." Wanda wiped tears of mirth from her eyes.

"You're just yanking my chain." Steve wasn't sure whether he was relieved or disappointed about Chloe's choice of reading material.

"Am I?"

"Chloe's not like that."

"Like what? Sexy?"

"She's a librarian."

"She's a woman. And don't you forget it."

At this rate, Steve wasn't likely to.

Bells. Chloe heard ringing bells. She groggily hit the button on her alarm clock before realizing it was the phone ringing.

It was barely eight in the morning. It felt much earlier because of her restless night, consumed with outrageous dreams about a half-naked Steve draped over the hood of a car, with her right there beside him. His hands beneath her demure T-shirt, her legs wrapped around his lean hips, her hands sliding into the back pockets of his jeans to tug him closer…

She blinked, forcing herself to erase all memory of those forbidden thoughts as she grabbed for the phone.

"Hello?" she said huskily.

"Be ready in fifteen minutes." Steve sounded wide awake, his deep voice authoritative.

"Ready for what?"

"For me."

It would take her hours to get ready for him but she wasn't about to tell him that. Despite his assurances during their dinner last night, a tiny part of her had expected him to make a move on her when they'd gotten home. But he hadn't.

Which was a good thing. It proved they were a team, not a couple. There was no grand passion here. At least not on his part. And not on hers, if she knew what was good for her.

"Put on some jeans and a T-shirt," Steve was telling her. "We're headed for the open road."

"What are you talking about—"

"Fifteen minutes," he warned her. "The clock is running."

She opened her front door in exactly fifteen minutes to find Steve perched on his Harley. Flashing her a sexy grin, he patted the passenger seat behind him. "Hop on."

Chapter Five

"You want me to get on your motorbike?" Chloe's initial reaction was something along the lines of *Are you nuts?*

But then she reminded herself of her goal to live a more adventurous life.

"Motorbike?" Steve sounded outraged. "This is no mere motorbike. This is a *Harley.*" His voice was reverent now. "This baby is a work of art with the sweetest 1450 cc twin cam air-cooled pushrod engine anyone could imagine, not to mention the constant velocity carburetor or the dual rear shock absorbers. And we're not even talking about the laced wheels or whitewalls."

As she got closer, Chloe was more impressed with how good Steve looked wearing jeans, a simple white T-shirt and a worn brown leather bomber jacket. He had such a powerful presence, more powerful than any mere Harley could be.

"Look, I've even got an extra helmet for you." He gently plunked it on her head. "Okay, we're good to go. Hop on."

"But where are we going?"

"On an adventure."

She couldn't hear so well with the helmet on. That became less of a problem once he turned the Harley on. Chloe had no idea how "sweet" it was, but it was certainly loud.

Chloe took that leap of faith, slinging her leg up and over the bike so that she was in the passenger seat. A roar of the throttle had her nervously clutching onto Steve as they started moving.

Fast.

Or so it seemed to Chloe, who watched bungalows whiz by before closing her eyes and clamping her arms around his waist to prevent herself from falling off.

"Sweet, huh?" he shouted.

Not really. *Hot* came closer to the mark. Hot and dangerous. Her widespread legs were pressed tightly against his...well, his muscular derriere.

She'd never ridden on a motorbike before, let alone on a Harley with a sexy Marine. And she'd certainly never been so sexually wound up. The rumble of the Harley's engine created a vibration that...well, she had to admit that maybe it was sweet. It certainly was doing wild things to her. She could feel the excitement burning in her, surging in her veins until her entire body was flushed with it.

Her senses were throwing her into a turmoil. Questions zinged through her mind. And what about her hands? Where should she put them? They were on his abdomen, but they kept slipping down to his belt buckle.

She'd burrowed her arms beneath his jacket so her fingers were against his T-shirt. The cotton felt smooth and warm. Her hands didn't meet so she couldn't just clasp them together....

What was the proper etiquette in such situations? Probably just to hold on and pray.

It didn't occur to Chloe for some time that she still had no idea where they were going. She deducted from some of the road signs flashing by that they were headed north, away from the city.

Where was he taking her?

She wanted to ask him, but doing that required removing her cheek from his back and she wasn't prepared to do that yet. She considered herself quite brave to have managed to turn her head from side to side to see what they were passing.

Before too long, they were out in the countryside, beyond the suburban sprawl that seemed to collar the city for miles.

Or maybe she'd just lost track of time, being so engrossed as she'd been with the vibrating engine and Steve's sexy body and all.

Chloe tried hard to be analytical, attempting to allocate what percentage of her tumultuous feelings was caused by him and how much was caused by the Harley. But it was difficult to be rational when she was all churned up inside. She was experiencing so many different sensations she couldn't begin to catalog them all.

She was still trying to figure things out as they crossed the state line into Wisconsin. The farther north they went, the more vivid the fall foliage became. The greens of summer were replaced by the brilliant yellows and fiery reds. The leaves were even more intense against the deep blue sky.

Steve had avoided the expressways and had instead stuck to the back roads. He seemed to know where he was going. But then men were good at that, acting like they knew their way, when they didn't have a clue.

She'd read a book about that, about the different communication styles between men and women, about their reasons for refusing to ask for directions. But darned if she could remember the details at the moment. She kept being distracted by the here and now. Like how good Steve smelled—part leather, part clean soap, part just plain male.

She sat a little straighter and tried to peer over Steve's shoulder. That didn't work, he sat too tall. Maybe if she moved a little to one side…

Chloe did and panicked when the bike seemed to tilt as if in danger of falling over.

She returned to her former position and scooted even closer. Her hands slipped again, this time all the way down to the placket of his jeans.

Steve took one hand off the handlebars to move her hands back up to his chest.

Chloe was mortified. She hoped he didn't think she was trying to cop a feel or anything. Her face burned and she was glad he couldn't see her, although she would have liked to explain that her hands had just slipped. She suddenly recalled seeing some helmets that had microphones attached to them, presumably so driver and passenger could speak to one another. She certainly didn't want him thinking her hands were doing the talking.

But her helmet had no microphone.

She forced her attention to the passing scenery as a

way to get her thoughts headed in another direction. Eventually that tactic worked because the pastoral surroundings were not only pretty, but they were also peaceful. Wooded ridges and gumdrop-shaped hills created a bucolic landscape. Well-tended farms with red barns and silver-capped silos dotted the countryside. Large wooded areas of oak, maple and hickory provided bursts of color.

As a little girl, Chloe had read a storybook about Jack Frost gleefully coating the leaves before spilling buckets of color over a hillside.

That's how it looked right now. The big red and gold trees were splashy and bold. Autumn was her favorite season, the ever-changing weather could bring the remembered warm sunshine of summer one day and the threat of wintery showers the next.

It was only now occurring to her that it was interesting that her favorite time of year was the one with the most vivid living-color displays.

If she'd liked bland, why choose autumn?

Sure there were some trees whose leaves simply turned brown and fell to the ground, but there were so many others that put on a spectacular show.

She'd been in danger of becoming one of those brown leaves, but she wanted to be one of the rowdy sugar-maple leaves—the tricolored kind with shades of green, yellow and finally red.

Yes, Chloe wanted to be one of the bright chromatic ones that people collected and carefully pressed into books to save. Not the brown ones that people crumpled beneath their feet or that sat there and turned into mulch.

This was her first step toward that goal—living a more adventurous life. Living in the moment.

They traveled through a valley and up another hill before she noticed that Steve seemed to be slowing down.

Now he was turning, into a farm stand.

Well, it actually appeared to be bigger than a farm stand since it was located in a rustic barn. Square bales of hay were placed artistically around, along with rows of yellow mums and pumpkins. There was even a scarecrow, wearing a plaid flannel shirt and denim overalls, seated in a rustic wooden wagon.

When they came to a stop, Steve braced one leg on the graveled ground.

Chloe wasn't sure how she dismounted, if that was the proper term, from the Harley, but once she did so, she noticed her legs felt all rubbery. Was that Steve's fault or his beloved motorbike's?

"I thought we could use a break," he said, removing his helmet to face her.

"Good idea." Why did her voice sound all croaky?

"You can take your helmet off now. Want some help?"

She needed help, all right, but not from the source of her trouble. "No, I'm fine."

She may have been fine but her fingers weren't. They were all thumbs as she struggled to get the strap undone.

"Here." Steve nudged her hand aside and took care of things himself.

It wasn't the first time she'd noticed how gentle his touch could be for such a powerful man. He had large hands. His fingers were long and lean, his nails clean and closely clipped. But there was more than just the physical description at work here. These were a warrior's hands, capable of defending and protecting. Also capable of making her knees go all funny.

"There." He stepped back. "Better, huh?"

"Infinitely." At least she could still utter four-sylla-ble words, even if only one at a time. She firmly slid her black-framed glasses back into place.

"Good. I thought we could pick up some food for a picnic lunch over at Devil's Lake."

Seemed an apt destination for a man as sexy as the devil.

And Chloe was hungry. Starving actually. She'd only had time to grab a granola bar before leaving the house that morning.

As they approached the building, the sun glinted on bushel baskets full of ruby, gold and green apples. The display was set out on tables along with signs listing the varieties—Granny Smith, Yellow Delicious, Jonathan. And, of course, there was a section inside the barn it-self with a deli offering an incredible variety of cheese. After all, they *were* in Wisconsin. Even their football fans up here were called "cheeseheads."

"Wisconsin is the number-one cheese producer in the nation, you know. They produce 2.5 billion pounds annually." Jeez, she couldn't believe she'd just spouted statistics at him. She only did that when she was really nervous. She had all kinds of trivia stored in her mind. It went with the job, which often had her looking up all kinds of things—from the average annual rainfall in Belize to the lifespan of a grizzly bear.

"What do you think about some cheddar?" Steve held up a plastic-covered wedge.

"Sounds good." She looked around at the displays. "I can't believe they've got blueberry Monterey Jack cheese here."

"Why? Is that a favorite of yours?"

"I've never tasted it."

"We should try some then." He added it to the shopping basket she held.

Another section offered several varieties of sausage. "They have venison sausage," Steve noted.

"I am not eating Bambi in any shape or form."

"Not feeling that adventurous, huh? Okay, fine. No deer meat." He picked up a summer sausage instead.

When they returned to the Harley, Steve stored their purchases in the leather saddlebags along the backside of the bike. "Ready?"

She nodded. This time she felt more confident as she swung her leg over the passenger seat. She was becoming a biker babe.

The ride to Devil's Lake was a scenic one. The road twisted and climbed into a series of lush, wooded hills to the entrance of the state park.

A short while later, Steve pulled the Harley to a smooth stop in the parking lot. This time Chloe dismounted with an elegant grace that even she was proud of.

"You did good for a two-wheeled novice," Steve noted.

"What makes you think that I was a novice?" she countered.

"Oh, I don't know. Maybe the way you hung onto me for dear life."

"Maybe I was just doing that for effect."

It had had some kind of effect on him, that's for sure. Having her pressed up so closely against him, like white on rice, had made him very aware of her. Male to female. And then his heart had almost stopped when her hands had landed on the placket of his jeans.

They were supposed to be comrades in arms of bad luck in the romance department. A team. No sex involved. No desire to have sex included.

Steve took a deep breath and reassured himself that everything was under control. Because there was no way he was stepping back into that frying pan after having just stepped out of the relationship fire.

What was that phrase—once bitten, twice shy?

No, he didn't like the sound of that. No way was he shy. Smart. Once bitten, twice smart. Yes, he liked that better. He was smart. He learned from his mistakes. And never, ever repeated them.

Good. He had that straight then. He finished locking up his Harley before turning to find Chloe heading off. "Where are you going?"

She pointed to the nearby picnic table. "To eat."

Steve shook his head as he finished transferring their food into a backpack.

She lifted an eyebrow. "No?"

He shook his head again.

She waved a hand. "Then you pick which picnic table."

"We're not eating at a table."

"Then where are we eating?"

He pointed toward the bluffs surrounding the lake. "Up there. Not afraid of heights, are you?"

"Would it matter if I was?"

"Knowing what you're afraid of helps you overcome it. Those five-hundred-foot bluffs are among the most ancient outcrops on the planet. They're something like a billion years old." At her surprised look, he shrugged. "I did some recon ahead of time on the Internet about the place."

"Well, luckily I'm not afraid of heights." *Just sexy Marines.*

The renegade thought flashed through her mind. She

kept finding things they had in common, like the bit of trivia he'd just shared with her. Now she didn't feel so dumb about her earlier comments regarding Wisconsin cheese. But it did scare her a bit to realize how much she enjoyed his company.

"Come on." He linked her hand with his. "Let's go."

He wasn't really talkative during their hike, which was a good thing. Then he couldn't tell how breathless Chloe was.

It wasn't that she was that badly out of shape. She wasn't. She walked three miles several times a week with a group from her neighborhood. The Wannabe Walkers were a dozen strong, and included a diverse group of men and women from young moms to senior citizens.

But her walks with them didn't resemble this one with Steve at all. For one thing, they didn't hold hands. And even if they had, she wouldn't have been faced with the unexpected dilemma of enjoying it so much she didn't want to break off the contact.

"I see the perfect place for our lunch…." He led her to a perch on top of one of the bluffs with a beautiful view. The rocks reared up above the surrounding land while the lake sparkled below in the sunlight. Natural rock formations created a table for them to spread out their feast of apples, cheese, crackers and sausage.

"This is better than settling for some dull picnic table, isn't it?" Steve said.

Was that what she'd been doing with her life lately? Chloe wondered. *Settling?* Accepting the dullness instead of striking out on a new, exciting path that might end with a great view.

Or it could end with you falling right off the bluff, her conservative inner voice noted.

Face it, she'd never been one to take risks. Not since her parents had died. They hadn't been big risk takers either, but Janis had never let her forget that their last risk had taken their lives. "If they hadn't decided to charter that private plane for their anniversary trip, they'd still be alive today." *And I wouldn't be stuck with you,* was unspoken but always there in Janis's sharp voice.

No one could have been sorrier than Chloe that her parents were no longer with her. She still missed them.

"Are you ready?" Steve's voice interrupted her thoughts.

"Ready?"

"To eat." While she'd been lost in memories, he'd sliced the apples with his Swiss Army knife.

When Steve offered her a piece of the juicy fruit, it occurred to her that this was a role reversal from the Garden of Eden. Steve was the one leading her into temptation.

She was at a fork in the road of her life. She could either stay on the well-worn dull path or she could continue to explore new territory. Resist or accept? She reached out and took the apple he offered.

"So you've never been up here before?" Steve asked.

She shook her head.

"It's a popular place for people living in Chicago to visit."

"I haven't always lived in Chicago."

"No?"

She shook her head. "My parents lived there but after their death I went to live with Janis. My mom's older sister."

"The aunt you said you weren't close to."

"She didn't want me calling her aunt."

"Why not?"

"She told me she didn't feel like anyone's aunt so I should call her Janis." Chloe paused to take a bite of apple. "I'd never actually met her before living with her. She wasn't that close to my mom, but she was her only living relative. Anyway, Janis lived near MIT in Massachusetts. I went to live with her when I was eight."

"That must have been tough."

"When I turned twelve, Janis sent me off to boarding school until I turned eighteen. I really only lived with her for four years, from the age of eight to twelve." But those four years had made a huge impression.

"How did you like boarding school?"

"How did you like boot camp?" she retorted.

"Boot camp is meant to tear you down in order to build you up again."

"Sounds like boarding school. They were great at the tearing down part, not so good at the building up. I survived by escaping into books. The school did have a wonderful library and a nice librarian. I read everything I could get my hands on. The books would transport me from my dismal surroundings to Regency England or Napoleonic France. I could solve a cozy mystery along with Miss Marple or find adventure with the Three Musketeers."

"You like history?"

"I like reading. History, biographies, psychology, home decorating, all kinds of things. Opening a book is like opening a portal into another world." She paused, belatedly realizing how much of herself she'd just revealed. "I'm sorry, I didn't mean to hog the conversation that way."

"You weren't. I was interested."

"Your turn now. Tell me about yourself. What's it like having a twin?"

"We're not identical twins." Steve cut two more apples.

"I know. Your grandmother has shown me pictures."

He flashed her a grin. "Then you know that I'm the good-looking one in my family."

"All five Kozlowski brothers seemed good-looking from their photographs."

He airily waved her words away. "Those were touched-up photos."

She tried hard not to laugh. "Oh really?"

He nodded solemnly. "In reality, they don't look anything like those photographs."

"So you're even better looking than your twin?"

"Tommy is okay, I guess. Plenty of females seem to think so. Not as many as admire me, of course."

"Of course. What about your older brothers?"

"They're all married," Steve said.

She gave him a quizzical look. "You say that as if warning me off them."

"That's not what I meant. I meant that Tom and I are the only two remaining Kozlowski bachelors."

"Are you and you brother stationed together?"

Steve shook his head, his expression turning serious. "No, he's in the Middle East right now."

"Do you worry about him?"

"He knows how to take care of himself."

"You still haven't said what it's like having a twin."

"It's no big deal. Seems normal to me. It's all I've ever known."

"Do you have any kind of special connection?"

Steve did, but he wasn't about to admit that. It sounded too weird. There was that time when they were kids and

Tommy's appendix had ruptured. Steve had felt the pain, too. Or then there was the time they'd both come down with chicken pox at exactly the same moment.

A more recent occurrence was the fact that they'd both purchased the same model Harley without consulting one another beforehand. Stuff like that.

"I can't imagine what it would be like to have a sibling," Chloe was saying as she reached for another cracker and slice of cheese. "Let alone one who's a twin. It must be nice not to feel so alone."

"Were you lonely at boarding school?"

"I never really fit in there. I didn't seem to fit in anywhere until I went to college. Then I was one of those geeky, nerdy types. Always had a book in my hand, and several more in my backpack."

"Well you aren't geeky or nerdy now. What did you think of your first time?"

She almost choked, wondering if he was asking her if she was a virgin. "My…first…time?"

He reached around her to pat her on the back as he had in her kitchen the other day. Then he handed her the bottle of water. She took several sips before nodding to indicate she'd recovered.

"Your first time on a Harley? Why? What did you think I was asking you?"

She wasn't about to answer that question. The truth was that she *was* still a virgin. It wasn't something she broadcast to anyone. But she'd been telling the truth about being a nerd even in college. She'd had male friends, but had never wanted to have sex with any of them. They hadn't seemed to want to have sex with her either.

Maybe the bottom line was that she was an old-fashioned girl, wanting to wait until she found a man she loved enough to marry, to spend the rest of her life with, before she shared that intimacy with him.

Her thoughts returned to the present, belatedly answering his question. "My first ride on a Harley was quite memorable."

"In what way?"

Chloe wasn't about to tell Steve how being so close to him had just about made her go up in hormone-induced flames. Instead she said, "It's different than riding in a car."

"I should think so. The helmet gets in the way of the real experience, when it's just you, the sky, and the road. The experience is all around you. But I've seen what happens when you don't wear a helmet. Not a pretty picture."

"So you *can* be cautious," Chloe noted.

"Affirmative."

"That's a step toward your goal then, of learning to be more cautious. Being a Marine, it's probably natural that your inclination is that of a risk taker."

"Marines are risk technicians. We know the risks and are able to manage them because of training and knowledge."

"That sounds sensible."

"Yeah, that's me. Just a regular sensible kind of guy. Why that face?" he demanded. "You don't believe me?"

"Not really."

"Why not?"

"Where should I begin? There are so many reasons. A sensible guy wouldn't have whisked me off to Wisconsin for the day."

"It seemed like a sensible plan of action to me."

"That's the point. You have your own way of looking at things, of doing things."

"I should hope so. I've had years of training. I'm expected to lead men who consider themselves to be as tough as nails. Which means I have to be able to do everything they can do and more. That's why I'm a captain in the United States Marine Corps."

"So you can boss other people around?"

"It's called ordering, not bossing, and no that's not the reason. As you know, my dad was a Marine as are all my brothers so I'm following in a time-honored tradition. You said you like history. Well, the Marine Corps is the most history-conscious of all the services. On November 10th, 1775, the Continental Congress passed a resolution establishing the Continental Marines and marked the birth date of the United States Marine Corps. November 10th is a birth date that is still celebrated by the Marine Corps to this day. This proud heritage is part of the Marine Corps culture that I admire."

"Honor, courage, commitment." She smiled. "I've done a bit of research myself. After all, that is what I do for a living as a reference librarian."

"Our jobs really do have certain similarities, you know."

"Really?"

"Absolutely. We're both used to maintaining order and control. And we're both into problem solving."

"I never thought of it that way."

"I'm a lean, mean fighting machine. You're a lean, mean reading-and-research machine. You know, I'm surprised no one's developed an action figure for librarians yet."

Chloe laughed. "Actually someone has. There's a

site on the Internet that has them. Has them *shh*ing everyone. Which is a stereotypical cliché, of course."

He nodded solemnly. "I've never once heard you *shh*ing me."

"Of course not."

"Or told me, 'Silence please.' Or 'Quiet please.' Or told me to put a sock in it."

"Right."

"Although you've said it with a look," Steve added.

"What are you talking about?" she demanded.

"That look you have. Actually you have several. One is like this." He tried to demonstrate. "Then you can ratchet it up a notch with the explosive one." His expression became more dramatic as he wrinkled his forehead and narrowed his eyes. "Now that differs from what we Marines use for discipline. We have our war faces." He wiped all expression from his face, which hardened him.

"I'm impressed."

He ruined the effect by grinning. "Good."

But as the day went on, Chloe wondered if it really was good to be impressed by him. Then she reminded herself that she was supposed to be living in the moment and not overthinking everything. It was during one of these internal conversations that her attention drifted from the path in front of her, making her stumble over a slightly protruding rock.

She felt herself falling forward before Steve caught her.

Their surroundings fell away as Chloe found herself in the circle of his arms. Being this close to him, she noticed the tiny lines at the corners of his green eyes, his well-shaped eyebrows and the dark fringe of his surprisingly long eyelashes. He was a man of many facets, strong yet capable of gentleness, considerate yet demanding.

And he had a way of making her feel terribly young and inexperienced at times like this. He projected tons of confidence in his relationship with the world, and with the women in his world. That sureness showed in the way he carried himself, the way he moved with a certainty and a pride that was second nature to him. He seemed to have the ability to adapt himself, whatever his surroundings. On the back of a Harley, hiking atop a ridge in Wisconsin, eating *kolachkis* in his grandmother's kitchen.

She wondered if the Marine Corps had provided him with that powerful presence or if it was part of his inherent nature. She suspected it was a combination of both things.

"Are you okay?"

She nodded, noting that even his voice was powerful with a deepness that rumbled in his chest. Why hadn't she noticed that before? Maybe because she hadn't been standing so close to him that she could practically *feel* him speak.

Time to return to the real world and her own two feet. They were a team, not a couple. She moved away. "Yes, I'm fine. Thanks. Sorry for being so clumsy."

"No problem."

Right. No problem. Because this was teamwork, the two of them working together without getting bogged down in any of that romantic stuff.

During the ride home, Chloe was distracted by the spectacular sunset that glowed above them as they traveled down the road. The world felt all sky, from horizon to horizon.

It had been a perfect day. She couldn't remember the last time she'd had this much fun. Maybe she'd *never* had this much fun before. Happiness glowed within her.

Darkness had fallen by the time Steve pulled the Harley into her driveway. Her porch light cast enough illumination for them to see.

She got off the bike and swayed a bit, trying to regain her land legs after riding for so long.

"Steady there." Steve placed his hands on her shoulders.

Chloe placed her hands on his chest.

Slow and easy, he pulled her closer. She went.

The look he gave her made it clear that he was giving her a choice. Stay or step away.

Her decision came from the heart. There was no logical basis for her actions. She was being driven by forces beyond her control. The ride on the Harley had led up to this moment. Everything, every touch, every look, every moment had been building to this one.

Cupping her chin with one hand, Steve lifted her face to his. He lowered his head while gently brushing his thumb just once across her lower lip.

Chloe still had time to pull back from the edge, but she was too tempted to stop now. She closed her eyes, anticipation making her heart race.

What if it wasn't as she imagined? What if she bumped her nose against his? What if there was no magic? What if, what if…

The panic came too late and was erased the instant his lips covered hers.

Steve was wrong. His Harley wasn't sweet. His *kiss* was.

Chapter Six

The Marine sure knew how to kiss. He started out slowly, inviting her to share her secrets with him. He didn't inundate her, didn't capture her with anything but the sheer pleasure of his mouth brushing back and forth across hers.

There was no bossiness here, only a seductive request to participate. The zing-zing she'd felt the very first night she'd met him was amplified a hundredfold. There was no rush to increase the passion. Instead every second was drawn out and filled with anticipation and appreciation.

When Steve finally coaxed her lips to part, she was more than ready. The first touch of his tongue took things to a new level. Now his kiss became both dangerous and exhilarating. Passion drove her closer, steering her into a headlong collision between restraint and recklessness.

What was she doing? What was going on here? Had he simply kissed her good-night to be polite? Had she misunderstood and melted in his arms like a love-starved bookworm? She was teetering on the edge of something she hadn't anticipated.

She stepped away from the precipice. She stepped away from him. Steve let her go without complaint.

Even though Chloe wanted to run inside to the comfort of her house and her books, she forced herself to stay and smile at him. "I had fun today." She was so thankful that her voice sounded cheerful and not desperate.

"I'm glad."

As Chloe made her dignified exit, she was aware of Steve watching her, but she was even more aware that this had been one of the best days of her life. She just wasn't sure if that was a good thing or not.

"We're going out for lunch," Lynn told her the minute Chloe stepped foot into the library on Monday morning.

"We are?"

"Yes, we are. So that you can tell me everything that happened on Saturday night. I tried calling you several times yesterday but I only got your machine."

"I'm sorry, I was out all day."

"All day?"

"Yes. We went up to Wisconsin for the day and by the time we got home, it was too late to call you."

"We?"

Chloe nodded.

"As in Steve and you?" Lynn asked.

Chloe nodded again.

"We are definitely having lunch."

Chloe had a hard time concentrating throughout the busy morning. Her thoughts kept straying to her day with Steve and that kiss they'd shared last night. It took more effort than usual to focus on her work, but she managed to do so whenever a patron came to the reference desk for assistance or whenever she answered a phone call.

She answered such diverse questions as *When did Seabiscuit win his last race?* and *What's the name of the river under the Ponte Vecchio?* That last one was from the *Chicago Tribune* crossword puzzle and so she was asked that question a number of times. Polish Heritage Month was coming up October first, so she had a number of requests for information on that and inquiries about the Polish book club that read works in their native language. Wanda was a frequent participant in that. Plus Chloe was responsible for the nonfiction book display for the week, which meant she had to gather the materials for the glass case near the entrance door.

She'd selected Fall Foliage as her topic. She gathered a variety of books—from the scientific explanation of why leaves change color to photographic coffee-table tomes. A small toy squirrel in one corner along with a child's plastic rake in the other provided additional interest. She'd even gathered some of the more colorful leaves from her own backyard and included those, some stapled to the back of the case, some artistically strewn around the bottom.

She had a few leaves she'd picked up at Devil's Lake, but she had most of those tucked into a book at home for pressing, with one stuck into the edge of her dresser mirror. Mementos of her perfect day with Steve.

With so much to do, Chloe couldn't get away for lunch until almost one.

She and Lynn walked to Paco's Tacos around the corner. Since they were frequent customers, the owner, Paco, greeted them with a smile. "The usual, ladies?"

They nodded.

A few minutes later, they took their order to one of the dozen tables and sat down. Chloe's "usual" was a taco salad and Lynn had the cheese-and-veggie quesadillas. They both had diet sodas and shared an order of salsa and chips.

"Okay, tell all," Lynn said. "Start with Saturday night."

"We went to this great restaurant in Lincoln Park. It was decorated in the Arts and Crafts-style and it had the most gorgeous views of the park and the city. And the food was incredible."

"Did he kiss you when he took you home?"

"No, of course not. He was a perfect gentleman. Besides, we'd only gone out to discuss his plan to make his grandmother think that her matchmaking efforts for the two of us were successful."

"Right. And what about all day Sunday?"

"The same thing. I'd never ridden on a Harley before...."

"He has a Harley?"

Chloe nodded and then picked a hot jalepeño pepper off her salad. Paco must have put it on there by mistake. He knew she didn't like her salad too spicy.

"A Harley? And you rode it?" Lynn shook her head with admiration. "You wild woman, you."

"I wore a helmet."

"Oh, that makes it okay then." Lynn tossed a corn chip at her. "Did you have fun? Where did you go?"

"I had no idea where we were going at first," Chloe admitted.

"He didn't tell you?"

"No, he just showed up and told me to hop on his Harley. That's not exactly true, he did call me first to tell me that he was outside my house."

"And you got on his bike, without knowing where he was taking you?"

Chloe nodded.

"That doesn't sound like you."

"It's time I had some adventures. Took some chances."

"I thought you didn't want to take chances after what happened with Brad."

"Not *romantic* chances. But this is just for fun."

"Right. Fun."

"Yes. Fun. Something I don't have all that much experience with. But I'm doing better. By the end of the day I could hop off that Harley like a regular biker babe."

"It couldn't have been very comfortable."

"It wasn't too bad."

"The inner muscles on your thighs aren't sore from straddling that bike?"

"I'm more sore from the hike we took to the bluffs above Devil's Lake. We had a picnic up there. It was great."

"It sounds like it." Lynn smirked.

"What?" Chloe demanded.

"Nothing. I'm just happy that you had a nice time. And wondering what you'll be doing next? Hang gliding? Bungee jumping?"

"No, but I always have wanted to go hot-air ballooning."

"You're kidding, right?"

"No." Chloe took a sip of her soda. "That's something I've always wanted to do, but never quite had the nerve."

"And now you do have the nerve?"

Chloe grinned. "I'm getting there." With a little help from a Marine named Steve.

"How was your day yesterday?" Wanda asked Steve Monday afternoon. She'd spent the morning at some kind of women's church-group meeting so she hadn't had a chance to interrogate Steve until now.

"Outstanding. I took Chloe up to Wisconsin on the Harley. We had a great time."

"Really?"

"Absolutely."

"I'm so glad to hear that."

Steve refused to feel guilty at the delighted look on his grandmother's face. He wasn't lying to her. He *had* taken Chloe up to Wisconsin. They *had* had a great time.

But he was misleading his Busha into thinking that anything could come of this Alpha Libras mission.

What about that kiss last night? Why had he kissed her? What had he been thinking? Steve had started asking himself more questions than even his grandmother did.

The answer was simple. He'd kissed her because he'd wanted to.

Simple? Yeah, right. There was nothing simple about this situation.

What happened to being smart and learning from his mistakes? So his mistake had been what? Falling for Gina? Trusting his backstabbing buddy? Which meant what, that he could never trust another friend again? That he could never trust another female again? Of course not.

Okay, so yes, he had fallen for Gina quickly. And that bitter lesson had taught him that he needed to proceed with caution instead of rushing headlong into anything. Obviously that was easier said than done, given the fact that he'd always been the one who rushed into things. Tommy was the one who stood back and weighed his options.

But he could change. That was part of this mission. He was to teach Chloe how to be more adventurous and she'd teach him to be more cautious where relationships were concerned.

He'd been stupid to agree to that. How could she teach him to be cautious when she kissed him back so passionately? He should just focus on training her to be more adventurous. Like boot camp.

He remembered her soft voice talking about her experiences at boarding school and comparing it to boot camp. They weren't the same, of course. Boot camp trained you to become a warrior. You were taught how to wage war and how to manage peace.

A sudden nudge in his side returned his attention to his petite Busha. "Where did you go? I was talking to you and suddenly you were off somewhere else. In another world. You were thinking of Chloe, yes?"

"I was thinking of your *kolachkis.*"

"Oh you!" She socked his arm. "I want to see you happy. I want to see you married and settled."

"I'm a Marine. We never get settled."

She waved his words away. "You know what I mean."

"Did you try this hard to hook Rad up with his fiancée?"

"He was already engaged when I went to visit him in North Carolina. And yes, I know now that the engagement was not real at that time. But his love for Serena is real now. That's what I want for you."

"That's nice of you, but there's no rush."

"You won't be on leave forever," Wanda reminded him.

"Let's just take things one day at a time for now, okay?"

Steve felt like an idiot, hanging around the library entrance, trying to figure out what he was going to say to Chloe. The truth was he was still recovering from their kiss last night. She hadn't seemed all that affected, smiling at him and telling him she had a fun time before calmly walking into her house.

Could it be that the librarian was used to kisses like that? He didn't want to think so. He didn't like the image of her in some other guy's arms.

He'd had a great time with her yesterday. He hadn't expected her to be as open to just taking off to Wisconsin the way they had. He'd gotten a real kick out of being the one to show her how to have fun.

That's all this was. Fun. Nothing serious. Not on his part for sure. But that kiss…well, that hadn't been in his game plan.

Steve saw Chloe before she saw him. She was walking toward the library with another woman. She was back in her librarian persona, wearing a conservative pair of khaki pants and a sweater. The sweater was red, though, and brightened up her face. Several tendrils of her dark hair had come undone from her ponytail and curled around her face. Her glasses had slipped down her nose so she absently pushed them back into place while animatedly talking to someone who was obviously a friend.

"Hi, there."

"Steve!" Her smile was startled but pleased. "I wasn't expecting to see you here."

"I was in the neighborhood and thought I'd drop by."

Lynn cleared her throat. Chloe made the introductions.

"We were just talking about you," Lynn told Steve.

He raised an eyebrow. "You were?"

Chloe elbowed Lynn into silence. "I was just telling her how spectacular the fall colors were up in Wisconsin."

Steve's grin indicated that he didn't believe one word. "Right."

"Well, I'll leave you two alone then," Lynn said with a bright smile.

Chloe wanted to point out that they were hardly alone, standing as they were at the library's main entrance. But she remained quiet instead and waited for Steve to speak first. She didn't have to wait long.

"I thought I should warn you that my grandmother is going to invite you over for dinner on Wednesday," he said.

"That's nice of her."

"To meet my parents."

"Uh-oh."

"We should talk about it over dinner tonight, unless you've got other plans?"

"No, I don't have any other plans."

"Good. When should I pick you up?"

"Um, six-thirty? Is that too early?"

"No, that's fine. I'll see you then."

"But let's go someplace local tonight, okay? Nothing fancy."

"Agreed."

They ended up at a local Chicago-style pizzeria.

Steve closed his eyes with pleasure at his first bite. It was so thick and juicy you had to eat it with a fork. Not like the skinny pizzas you got elsewhere. "You just can't get deep-dish pizza anyplace else like you get it here in Chicago."

"Why is your grandmother having me meet your parents?"

"Why do you think?"

"I think that maybe this is getting a little too serious."

"Nah." Steve waved her words away. "You haven't met my parents. They're not that serious. Well, my dad's a former Marine, so he does have this sort of tough exterior."

"I'm not good with parents." Her voice sounded small even to her.

"What do you mean?"

"I mean that I'm not good with parents." She tried not to hyperventilate. "I don't have a lot of experience in that department."

"You mean because your parents died when you were a kid?"

She nodded. This wasn't something she liked discussing, despite the fact that she'd told him all about her life when they'd had lunch above Devil's Lake yesterday. But parents…no, she just wasn't good meeting parents.

"Look, it's just a meal. No big deal."

"Then why did we have to meet tonight to prepare for it?"

"That was an excuse." His confession was accompanied by a slow smile. "I wanted to spend time with you."

Chloe didn't know how to respond. Neither one of them had brought up "the kiss." Chloe certainly wasn't going to be the first one to do so. Part of her wanted just to forget it had ever happened. The other part of her wondered when it would happen again.

A "fun girl" wouldn't take things so seriously.

"And I wanted pizza," Steve added, his smile turning into a grin. "I thought it would be nice having it with you."

Nice. Ah, yes, that was her middle name. *Nice. Boring. Dull.*

"Why the frown?" Steve asked.

"I was just thinking."

"Not a good idea."

"What?"

"Thinking. You do a lot of that. Take a break."

"I don't know if I can," Chloe admitted.

"Sure you can. You weren't thinking yesterday were you?"

"Not much, no." If she had, she wouldn't have let him kiss her.

"And that turned out okay, right?"

Okay? That ranked right up there with *nice.*

She had to stop making such a big deal about this. Steve was only in town for a short while. They were just hanging out together, having fun. Alpha Libras. A team, not a couple. Nothing serious. No romantic entanglements.

Then how did kissing get into the picture?

Well, it had been fun. Maybe she'd catalog it under that subject heading. Fun. Not romantic, even though it had been.

Maybe she should try thinking like a male. They didn't get all upset about kisses. They lived in the moment. Sure, why not? Easy for them to do that, they're not the ones who ended up with broken hearts.

She was so confused.

"You're thinking again." Steve reached for another slice of pizza. "I can hear you all the way over here."

"That's not possible."

"I'm a Marine. Anything is possible."

"So Marines are able to read people's thoughts now, hmm?"

"Affirmative. Especially when the aforementioned thoughts are written all over your face."

"Then what was I thinking?"

"That this is getting complicated. That maybe you shouldn't have agreed to do this."

Chloe refused to be impressed. "It doesn't take a mind reader to figure that out. I've said as much."

"Don't I get extra points for listening and remembering what you said?"

She had to laugh at his earnest expression.

"I like the sound of that." He brushed his fingers over the back of her hand.

"Are you flirting with me?"

"What do you think?"

"I think flirting is a bad idea."

"Because?"

"Because it…we…you…" she sputtered.

"Yes?"

"It just is."

"You look cute when you're serious."

She narrowed her eyes at him.

"Uh-oh, I recognize that look. It's the one you gave me at the library that first night. You know, I have to warn you that it might discourage some guys."

"That's my intention."

"Doesn't work on me though," Steve cheerfully added.

"Why not?"

"I don't get discouraged easily."

"How do you know I'm not like Gina? That I'm not some gold digger after your money?"

"You're not like Gina at all."

"Why? Because I'm not gorgeous and classy?"

"No, because you're not dishonest."

"You didn't think she was dishonest at first either. How can you trust your own judgment?"

"Ah, a valid point. It's hard after you've been betrayed, isn't it? Hard to face the fact that you made a mistake. That you were stupid."

"I didn't say you were stupid."

"Didn't you feel stupid after that guy dumped you?" She nodded slowly.

"But this situation is different. You and I are different. Because we're just...having fun together. Alpha Libras, right?"

"Right."

"We're a team."

"Right. That's what I told Lynn. She wondered if I was going to go bungee jumping next but I told her no, I'm not interested in that, although I have always wanted to ride on a hot-air balloon. Have you ever done that?"

Steve nodded. "Out in New Mexico once."

"How was it?"

"Slow."

"You're used to fast things like Harleys and F-16 jets, right?"

"Right."

Chloe wondered if he was used to fast women, too, but didn't have the nerve to ask.

"Are you ready for another piece of pizza?" Steve asked her.

She nodded and held out her plate. He'd just finished placing the bit of hot, stringy cheese onto her plate when they were joined by an older man standing beside their table. He had thick white hair and vivid blue eyes.

His attention was focused on Steve. "You'd be Wanda's grandson, then."

"That's right, sir. I'm Steve Kozlowski. And you are?"

"Interested in your grandmother."

Chapter Seven

Steve frowned at the older man. "Excuse me?"

"You heard me right enough." The guy's voice sounded defensive. "I'm interested in your grandmother."

"Interested in what way?" Steve wanted to make sure he understood what the stranger was trying to communicate.

"Interested in asking her out."

"And you're telling *me* this because?"

"Because I wanted to know your thoughts on it."

"My thoughts on you asking my grandmother out on a date? I don't even know who you are."

"My name's Patrick O'Hara and I'm the owner of this establishment and the tavern next door."

"How do you know my grandmother?"

"I live in the neighborhood. So what do you think?"

Steve looked down at his empty plate. "That you make a great deep-dish pizza."

Patrick frowned. "I meant about your grandmother."

"I don't know." Steve was at a loss. He'd never had a guy approach him and ask him about his grandmother. It felt weird. "Help me out here, Chloe. What do you think? Can you vouch for this guy?"

"He donated catering services for two of our library events this year," Chloe replied before giving Patrick a smile of gratitude.

Steve was not so easily impressed. "So he supports libraries. What else do you know?"

"That we get a lot of calls in the reference department from patrons at his tavern with bar bets, guys wanting to know how many calories are in beer or who invented the helicopter, things like that. But Mr. O'Hara is standing right here, so if you have personal questions, why don't you just ask him whatever you want to know?"

Steve shifted his attention back to the older man. "Have you served in the military?"

"United States Army. Four years. Korea."

The information made Steve relax a bit. The army wasn't as good as the Marine Corps, but still… The guy was a war veteran. "So you want me to put in a good word for you with my grandmother?"

Patrick nodded. "That's right."

"I suppose I can mention the fact that I ran into you this evening and that you asked about her. That you seem to run a tight ship in this eating establishment. You don't have a criminal record, do you?" Steve narrowed his eyes at him, sending him a warning look that had made young recruits tremble in their boots. "Because I have friends on the Chicago police force, so I can check that out."

Patrick showed no signs of bending, let alone trembling. "I have three sons and four grandsons on the Chicago police force. And no criminal record."

"That's good."

"Maybe you could put in a good word for me as well," Patrick suggested to Chloe. "Women tend to listen when other women talk to them."

"I'm curious, Mr. O'Hara." Chloe had to ask the question. "What makes you think that you need all this assistance before approaching Wanda yourself?"

"Well, we may have gotten off on the wrong foot."

"How so?" Chloe asked.

"There was this community thing. Some kind of spring fair several months ago. They had a bake-off and I was the judge in the dessert division. Wanda was a tad upset that I didn't give the blue ribbon to her *kolachkis*."

"That could be difficult to overcome," Steve told him. "Her *kolachkis* are famous."

"Mrs. O'Flaherty's brownies were better. In my opinion."

"Mrs. O'Flaherty, huh? Wouldn't be a case of you going with the Irish entry instead of the Polish one, now would it?"

Patrick drew himself to his full height and glared at Steve. "That's what your grandmother accused me of, and the answer is no. I didn't care who made the brownies." He paused, his irritation turning to exasperation. "Trust me, that's the last time I ever judge anything like that. Females tend to take things so personally."

Steve nodded in commiseration. "That's true."

"Hey!" Chloe kicked him under the table, not hard enough to do much damage but enough to get Steve's attention. "That was a totally sexist thing to say."

"But true," Patrick noted sadly.

"Maybe we should continue this conversation another time," Steve suggested with a pointed look at Chloe.

Patrick nodded. "Enjoy the rest of your dinner."

"I can't believe you said that," Chloe said once they were alone again.

"I can't believe you only left me one piece of pizza." He put it on his plate.

"Me? You asked me if I wanted another piece." Then it hit her. He was doing it again. "Don't try to distract me. It's not going to work this time."

He lifted an eyebrow. "Meaning it's worked before?"

"Once or twice. But I'm recognizing your modus operandi now." He seemed to enjoy goading her. She wasn't about to let him get away with it. But she couldn't let his comment go unanswered either. "Getting back to what you said earlier, women do not take things more personally."

He gave her a look that spoke volumes.

"Hey, we can be just as analytical as men. There are women in the Marine Corps now," she reminded him.

"Affirmative."

"Are you insinuating they aren't as good as the men?"

"I would never say something like that."

"Just think it, hmm?"

"No, not even think it. But female Marines have been trained to be tough."

"You want tough, try having a baby."

"I don't deny that women have their strengths."

"How generous of you."

"I meant to tell you that you showed some great interrogation techniques when you were talking to Patrick," Steve congratulated her. "You'd be good in intel."

"I wouldn't be too emotional?"

Steve sighed. "You're not going to let me hear the end of that, are you?"

"You're going to have to earn your way out of this one."

"And how do you suggest I go about doing that?"

"You're a creative guy." She took a bite of her pizza. "I'm sure you'll come up with something."

"I suppose trying to bribe you with chocolate would be useless?"

"You're welcome to try. But I don't intend to make it easy for you."

His wickedly disarming grin made her heart melt. "That's fine. Marines aren't into easy."

She wasn't about to let him off that quickly. "Neither are librarians."

"Yeah, I'm discovering that." His gaze now held an admiration that *really* did funny things to her insides.

"So maybe we are well matched after all."

"I'd say so."

"Which is good for Team Alpha Libras."

"Absolutely."

"And what's good for Team Alpha Libras is good for both of us, right?"

"That works for me." The humor in his green eyes belied the solemn expression he was attempting to keep on his face.

"Good."

A second later they were both laughing. Chloe wasn't even sure why. And she didn't care. She was having a good time. And as long as she kept her focus on the fun and not the romance, she'd be just fine.

Two days later, Steve stood in Chloe's foyer. "You're not nervous are you?"

"I wasn't until you asked me that," Chloe retorted.

"My parents aren't intimidating."

"You didn't have to come get me."

"I was afraid you might get cold feet."

Cold? There wasn't a single chilly cell in her entire body. On the contrary, she was all hot and bothered. And something inside of her was powerfully drawn to him, as if she were a magnet and he were true north.

Focus, she ordered herself. Stick with the program here. "Umm, I have some wine and some flowers. What did I do with them…?" Still distracted by how good Steve looked in his dark pants and crisp white shirt, she looked around the foyer for the hostess gifts she'd purchased. "They were here a minute ago."

"You look more upset than you did last night at that sushi bar."

Chloe wrinkled her nose at him. "I'm not that adventurous where my stomach is concerned."

"You did okay."

"I didn't expect a Marine like you to like sushi."

"I developed a taste for it when I was stationed over in Okinawa several years ago."

"Aha, there the flowers are. And the wine." She'd left them on the coffee table when she'd heard Steve at her front door. She reached for her coat. "I guess I'm ready to go then."

Steve took her coat from her. She wasn't accustomed to his old-fashioned manners. But she liked the way it made her feel. Special. Like she mattered.

She slid her arms into her wool coat and then shivered with unexpected pleasure as Steve freed her hair from the confines of the coat's collar. The brush of his fingertips against her nape created a jolt of awareness.

Startled, she almost dropped the bottle of wine before regaining a bit of her composure.

She quickly stepped away and turned to face him. He took the wine from her before holding the door open. "Have I told you how lovely you look?"

"No, and you don't have to."

"Hey, I say what I mean and I mean what I say."

She looked down at her outfit doubtfully. "I don't know. The skirt is kind of short…."

"That's why I like it." Steve's grin was deliciously wicked.

"I figured as much," she noted dryly.

It was the same black skirt she'd worn when they'd gone to dinner in Lincoln Park. This evening she'd teamed it with a red silk blouse. Red was a power color. Or so Lynn had told her that day she'd come over to help Chloe with her wardrobe.

"Let's go. We don't want to be late."

"Are we late? Why didn't you say something?" Now *she* was the one who hustled him out of her house.

"I'm so glad you're not nervous," he teased her.

"I just want to be punctual."

"Of course you do. It's what we all want, along with world peace."

She blew a raspberry at him.

"What?!" His astonishment was dramatically delivered by stepping back a few steps, jiggling the wine to clutch a free hand to his chest. "What is the world coming to when a librarian acts so recklessly?"

"You ain't seen nothin' yet," she assured him with a sexy sashay.

"So I'm discovering."

Chloe's burst of confidence lessened as she entered

Wanda's house and met Steve's parents. Not that they did anything to make her feel unwelcome or uncomfortable. On the contrary, Angela Kozlowski went out of her way to put Chloe at ease. She had vivid green eyes, so like Steve's, and short brown hair.

Wanda took the flowers and wine off to the kitchen in search of a vase and a corkscrew.

"I apologize if we seem a little out of it," Angela said. "My husband and I just returned from a trip up to Alaska yesterday."

Chloe had always wanted to go to Alaska. It was up there on her list along with going hot-air ballooning. "Did you go on a cruise?"

"No, we drove our RV. We've been going all over the country with it, but this was our longest trip so far."

"Do you live in the Chicago area?" Chloe asked before realizing she already knew the answer. Wanda had filled her in on everyone in the Kozlowski family over the years.

Angela nodded. "When we're not living in the RV, yes. We have a house a few miles from here which we're actually having major renovations done on right now. That's why Steve is staying here with his grandmother instead of at our house. But we've lived all over the country. It was only after Stan retired from the Marine Corps that we could think about the idea of settling down."

"They still don't have the concept down pat yet," Steve inserted. "Not when they're off gallivanting all over the country."

"It sounds like you lead an adventurous life." Chloe hoped she didn't sound too envious.

"I guess we do," Angela replied.

"It really got adventurous when we got a flat tire on

the Alcan Highway and there wasn't another vehicle in sight for miles and miles," Stan said.

"I thought it was more adventurous when you tried to take that photograph of a bear and got too close," Angela teased her husband. "We brought a few pictures."

Chloe smiled. She could see the affection in their teasing. "I'd love to see them."

"Don't worry, we won't bore you with tons of snapshots."

"I wouldn't be bored," Chloe assured Angela.

"No, I don't suppose you would be." Angela gave her a direct look, as if she had the ability to see into Chloe's very soul. "You don't seem like the kind of person who gets bored easily."

Chloe laughed self-consciously. "Just put a book in my hands and I'm a happy camper."

Angela nodded. "I know what you mean. I'm a reader myself. So is Stan."

"I raised my boys right," Wanda stated as she joined them in the living room. "Books are precious and are to be celebrated."

"I meant to tell you, we ran into someone the other night who asked about you, Busha," Steve said.

"Really?" Wanda set down some stuffed-mushroom hors d'oeuvres, moving aside one of her ceramic turtles from the coffee table. "And who might that be?"

"Patrick O'Hara. He owns—"

"I know what he owns and I know he has no taste!" Wanda stated emphatically.

"He was afraid you might still be holding a grudge about that blue ribbon."

Wanda lifted her chin with regal displeasure. "I do

not hold grudges. I am simply stating facts. The man has no taste. He didn't like my *kolachkis*."

Steve wrapped an affectionate arm around her. "I think he likes you, Busha."

Wanda sniffed, clearly unimpressed. "A man who doesn't like my *kolachkis* cannot possibly like me."

"He did like them—"

"Then he should have given them the blue ribbon and not to that Irish hussy who batted her false eyelashes at him and waved her brownies under his nose."

"Waved her brownies?" Stan was clearly lost.

"It was a bake-off contest," Steve explained to his dad.

"Oh." Stan nodded sagely. "Women get emotional over those kind of things."

Angela socked her husband's arm in exasperation. "How can you say that, Stan?"

He was unfazed by her reaction. "Because it's true."

Steve's look in Chloe's direction clearly said, *See? I told you so.*

"No more talk of this," Wanda stated firmly, smoothing the apron she wore. "You do not want to upset the cook before dinner."

"Is there anything I can do to help?" Chloe offered.

"You could try to convince my son and grandson that women are not emotional but I fear it would be a losing battle." Wanda paused a moment. "No, now that I think about it for a moment, we should not have to apologize for emotions. Emotions are a good thing."

"Not if you're a Marine," Steve said. "You check your emotions at the door and you do whatever it takes to get the job done."

"You don't think women can do this as well?" Wanda retorted. "Of course they can. How do you think your mother managed all those times your father was deployed overseas and she was left with five children to manage by herself? She checked her emotions and got the job done. Then she cried. There is nothing wrong with crying. You should try it some time."

Steve and Stan looked at her, clearly appalled by the very idea.

"It's okay." Angela patted her husband's hand. "We poor little emotional women won't make you cry tonight."

"Unless it's with pleasure at how tender my pork roast is." Wanda laughed, the sound ricocheting around the room.

The meal was a lesson in how the Kozlowski family worked. They didn't stand on ceremony. And for all their disclaimers about emotion, they did feel strongly about one another and about the things they cared about. The Marine Corps. Their country. Their honor. Their proud Polish heritage.

Added to the mix was the humor and the respect that clearly came across. Chloe could only sit back and admire it all. She'd never been a part of something like this before. A *family*.

Well, actually she had been part of a family, but then it had all gone away when her parents had died. The memories were bittersweet. The flash of her mother's smile, the deep rumble of her father's laugh.

She'd tried to hang on to the memories, clutching them like a lifeline as she'd lie awake in the narrow bed in her aunt's spare room. She'd take them out like treasured belongings and reverently explore them—her sixth birthday party with the balloons and clown, the platinum-blond-haired doll her father had given her "just because," the anticipation of waiting for Santa to come Christmas eve and leaving cookies and milk by the tree.

"Have some more potato pancakes." Wanda held the plate out for Chloe.

Chloe blinked and returned to the present. "No, thank you."

"You looked sad for a moment," Wanda noted in concern. "Is everything okay? No problems at work?"

Chloe shook her head. "Everything is fine."

"You enjoy working at the branch library, yes?" Wanda continued.

"Yes, I do. Every day is different. You never know what questions will come up, what patrons will ask. I'm a reference librarian, by the way," she added for Steve's parents' benefit.

Angela said, "You must be able to work well with people then."

Chloe hadn't really thought about that. "On a good day, hopefully I can do that."

"Wanda tells us you live next door?"

"That's right."

"These traditional Chicago-style bungalows are great," Stan noted. "I grew up in this house. My brothers and I had a great model train setup down in the basement. My dad worked for the railroads. A real blue-collar kind of guy. Very different from my wife's family and the way she grew up, on a huge ranch in Texas."

Sensing something in Stan's voice, Chloe didn't know what to say.

"And our sons grew up in ten different states," Angela said.

"But mostly in a state of chaos," Stan mocked.

"Chaos? No way. Not allowed in a Marine household. One thing all those moves did do was teach me how to pack efficiently," Angela noted with a laugh.

"I still haven't unpacked all my books and I moved in three years ago," Chloe confessed. "I've run out of space to put them all."

"You should have Steve help you put together some more bookcases. He did those for me." Wanda pointed to the wooden furniture in the corner of the dining room. "For my turtles."

"That's okay. They're very nice, but, really, I don't want him going to any trouble."

"Steve." Wanda nudged him with her elbow. "Tell her it would be no trouble."

"Has she always been this bossy?" Steve asked his parents.

"For as long as I can remember," Stan replied with a grin that matched his son's.

The rest of the evening went smoothly and Chloe enjoyed being part of a family, even if only for a short time.

"See, that wasn't so bad, was it?" Steve said as he escorted her back to her house next door.

"Your parents are nice."

"Just like me."

She laughed.

"What?" His expression was one of mock outrage. "You don't think I'm nice?"

"It's not the first word that comes to mind."

"Really? What is?"

Sexy. Tempting.

"What's the matter, cat got your tongue?"

"Meow."

"Hey, nice sound effects," he congratulated her.

"That wasn't me," Chloe indignantly denied.

"No?"

"No."

"Meow. Meow. Meooooow."

"Whoever it is sounds hungry." Steve hunkered down and looked around her garbage cans.

"What are you doing?"

"Recon. I have reason to believe there's a kitten around here. There you are. Come on, little guy, come on out. I'm not going to hurt you."

The sound of Steve's softly reassuring voice was almost her undoing.

"That's it, come on. It's too cold out here for a little guy like you, huh?" Steve patiently coaxed the kitten to come closer. "We'll take you inside and give you some dinner."

Chloe stood there frozen.

She hadn't had a pet since her parents had died. Her aunt had allergies and had handed Chloe's beloved cat Magik over to the Humane Society. Chloe had vowed then and there she'd never love another animal the way she had that cat. The pain of losing her had been too hard to take, especially on the heels of losing both her parents.

When she'd wept, Janis had accused her, "You'd think you loved that cat more than you did your mother and father."

More guilt. Chloe hadn't cried again after that. Not when Janis could see her.

But alone in her bed at night, sometimes the tears would seep from her eyes despite her best efforts to hold them back.

"No, I…" Her throat was clogged with emotion. "No, I can't have a kitten."

"Why not?"

"I…I work."

"A lot of people work, and they have kittens."

"It should go to a family that will love it."

"You can't love a kitten?"

Chloe didn't want to love a kitten. She didn't want to love anyone. Things never worked out.

Look what had happened with Brad. She thought she'd found Mr. Right.

Talk about living in a fantasy world.

At least with Steve, they were both on the same page. Bad luck in the romance department, wasn't that the way he'd put it? What if luck had nothing to do with it? What if there was something intrinsically wrong with her? Something that made her impossible to love? Something lacking.

Chloe blinked away the sudden threat of tears. Why was she getting so mushy and emotional?

Looking at the little kitten in Steve's arms, Chloe tried to be tough. She tried to harden her heart. She tried to be logical. To remain in control.

Oh, who was she kidding?

She couldn't turn away from a tiny creature in need if her life depended on it. She knew firsthand too much about being lost and alone in the world. Sure, she'd had Janis present in her life, but not really, not emotionally.

What if she ended up turning out like Janis? Wrapped up in her work, unable to relate on any kind of a personal level. Unable to love.

That thought scared Chloe more than the threat of having her heart broken again.

"Here, take her." Steve handed the kitten over to her.

Chloe took the purring but nervous animal and cuddled her against her breast. She could feel her defenses crumble.

Talk about an "aha" moment. Standing there on her back steps, with Steve beside her, and a kitten purring against her, Chloe had a revelation.

Wanda had told her about the turtles—about how they had to stick their necks out to move anywhere. They had to take risks. Or they went nowhere.

That was Chloe. She'd been a turtle since Brad had cheated on her. It was time to stick her neck out and move on.

"Give me your keys," Steve said, "and I'll open the back door."

"They're in my coat pocket."

A minute later, Chloe found herself seated at her kitchen table, the kitten purring on her lap.

"I'll be back in a few minutes," Steve told her before hightailing it out of her house.

Great. Chloe had just reached a possibly life-altering realization and the man partly responsible for it takes off as if his feet were on fire.

"I've still got you, though, hmm?" The kitten nuzzled closer. "You're such a little sweetie, aren't you? Maybe that's what I should call you. Sweetie. That's kind of sappy and sentimental, isn't it?" She scratched the kitten under its chin. "Too bad. I could name you something literary like Shakespeare, but I don't feel like it. Or you could be Sweetie Shakespeare." The kitten licked Chloe's hand. "You like that name, huh?"

Totally entranced, Chloe just sat there getting acquainted with the kitten. She'd have to go out and get a few cat supplies before too much longer. But that would mean moving the kitten who'd just fallen asleep on Chloe's lap, its little chin resting on Chloe's wrist.

The kitten blinked sleepily when Steve showed up at the back door with a large shopping bag in hand.

"Hey little guy, how's it going?"

"This kitten is not a guy. She's a girl."

"Not surprising. Another female who finagles her way into my heart." He rubbed the kitten's ear, making her purr ten times louder.

"You like animals?"

"Sure, who doesn't?"

Brad didn't. Janis didn't. Chloe had tried to keep her distance, but who could resist a little face like Sweetie's?

Chloe had forced herself to keep her distance for many years now. Sure, she donated money to the Anti-Cruelty Society or the Humane Society to help animals, but doing that had never required making an emotional commitment. She only hoped she was up to the task. Meanwhile, she was trying not to think about the fact that caring about something meant giving it the power to hurt you.

Instead she focused her attention on Steve. "So what's in the bag?"

"Supplies." He took them out to show her. "Chow." He set the bag of kitten food on her kitchen table. "A cat dish and a kitty litter box complete with a pooper-scooper. Last but not least, kitty litter."

"You went to go buy all this?"

"Well, sure. Where did you think I was going?"

"I don't know."

"I told you I'd be back in a few minutes."

She nodded. "I know, but…"

"I already told you that I say what I mean and I mean what I say."

She nodded again, nervously rubbing her chin against the top of Sweetie's head.

"You think I'd dump a kitten on you and walk out?"

Chloe didn't know what to think. She only knew what she was *feeling*…. Entirely too much for this Marine with the sexy grin and an apparent heart of gold.

Chapter Eight

"So what have you named her?" Steve was asking Chloe.

"Sweetie Shakespeare."

"I don't know." He gazed down doubtfully at the little black kitten with a heart-shaped splash of white under her chin. "She doesn't look at all like Shakespeare. You sure you don't want to call her Harley?"

"After your motorcycle?"

"I've told you, it's not a mere motorcycle, it's a work of art."

"I know, I know. With a sweet pushcart engine—"

"Pushrod!"

He sounded so insulted she just grinned. It was fun to be the one pushing his buttons for a change. "Right."

"She still shows no respect," Steve complained to Sweetie. "After all I've done for her."

"Yes, you have a tough life," Chloe returned in the same teasing manner. "You're so underappreciated."

"You've got that right."

"No one understands you."

"Right again."

"Or how wonderful you are."

"Affirmative."

Acting on pure impulse, Chloe reached out to place the palm of her hand against his cheek. His skin was warm and slightly rough with a hint of stubble. "Thank you for everything."

Her hand slid down his cheek to his crisp white shirt. Grinning, she took a handful of the material to tug him closer so she could kiss his cheek. But somehow, she miscalculated something and her lips landed on the corner of his mouth.

Steve turned his head. Their kiss was for real now, no longer a teasing show of appreciation but a heated exploration of sensual pleasure. His mouth brushed hers with bold yet reverent strokes, coaxing her lips to part. The moment they did, his tongue joined hers in a slick reunion, creating an erotic dalliance of sultry taste and touch.

Murmuring his approval, he explored every curve and corner of her mouth, pausing in between to gently catch her bottom lip between his teeth, drawing it into his mouth to suck and nibble until her sighs became moans of excitement.

Yeow!

Sweetie's yodel of disapproval took Chloe by surprise, making her immediately back away.

"I'm feeling much more appreciated now," Steve noted with a grin. "Maybe not by Sweetie at the moment, but by her new owner."

Chloe looked away. "You never really *own* a cat."

"Sounds like you have some experience with cats."

"I had one when I was a kid."

"Then why were you so resistant about giving Sweetie a home?"

"I'd rather not talk about it."

Since her voice was strained with some unnamed emotion, Steve didn't push her. Instead he watched as she bent her head and focused her attention on the kitten.

You'd think that the more time he spent with Chloe, the less he'd be intrigued by her. But that wasn't turning out to be the case. Instead he continued to find her fascinating. And that wasn't usual for him.

In the beginning, he'd admired her spunk and she'd made him laugh. But now he was noticing other stuff— like her legs, or the way her face reflected her emotions, or the sparkle in her eyes when she laughed, or even the sound of her laughter. And that made him a bit nervous.

Sure it was okay to notice legs, that was almost an automatic response from a healthy male.

But little stuff like the sound of her laughter? That indicated what? Infatuation? That wasn't a word or a concept that had been in his vocabulary since he'd left puberty behind.

So what was going on here? Steve wasn't sure and he didn't like not being sure. Had he ever noticed the sound of Gina's laugh? Again, he wasn't sure.

Marines weren't meant to have doubts. Steve had been trained to determine the best possible outcome given any situation and to prepare for the worst.

He and Chloe were supposed to be comrades in arms in the bad luck romance department. Nothing more than that.

So why was he so shaken by their kiss?

Marines were meant to be stirred, not shaken.

Not that Steve wanted her stirring any kind of emotional feelings within him. He'd already been caught in the crosshairs of a deceitful female who'd torn his heart out and stomped it flat.

Chloe didn't seem like the heart-stomping type, but there were times when it was better to be safe than to be sorry, and he had a strong feeling this was one of those times.

So he made a quick goodbye and headed out the door, where freedom beckoned and complicated sentimental stuff like kittens and females with glasses could be left behind.

The next afternoon, Steve told himself he hadn't been a wimp for taking off last night and leaving Chloe with the kitten. After all, he'd provided plenty of supplies for them.

It wasn't as if he'd been afraid to deal with Chloe after kissing her, right? So why was he sitting here in Pat's Tavern, downing a bottle of beer in the middle of the day.

The sound of his cell phone prevented him from answering that question.

"Where are you?" Striker demanded.

Fed up with life in general, Steve growled, "None of your business."

"Which means you're someplace you shouldn't be."

"Wrong. There's no reason why I shouldn't be about to order a cheeseburger from Pat's Tavern."

"You're in a bar? Okay, what did the librarian do to you?"

"She didn't do anything. Can't a guy eat a simple meal without getting hassled?"

"No."

"I've got to go. My food is getting cold."

Steve switched his phone off and reached for the menu. Since he'd told his brother he was eating a cheeseburger, he felt the desire to eat one now.

Fifteen minutes later, his made-to-order burger arrived. So did Striker.

Steve looked at his brother in surprise. "What are you doing here? How did you get here?"

"The King Oil jet, and I'm here in Chicago for a business meeting. Thought I'd drop by and say hi since I was in the neighborhood. That burger looks good." Striker waved to the waitress. "I'll have one of those, and one of those, too." He pointed to the beer and the burger.

The woman, well in her fifties, grinned and beamed at Striker.

His older brother had always had that effect on females. Didn't matter what their age was. He got to them.

Not that Striker didn't have his dark side. As a former Force Recon Marine, he was accustomed to keeping secrets. Given that fact, he shouldn't be nosing into other people's business.

Steve told him so.

"Hey, as your oldest brother, I do have certain duties that I have to perform. One of them is checking up on you."

"I'm almost thirty. I'm a captain in the United States Marine Corps. I do not need checking up on."

Striker was totally unimpressed. "So what did the little librarian do that's got your shorts in a knot?"

"She's not a *little* librarian."

"Ah, you're defending her." Striker shook his head with mocking pity. "You're worse off than I thought."

"Why didn't you give me a heads-up that you were coming to Chicago?"

Striker grinned. "I didn't want you taking off on that Harley of yours before I got here."

"Yeah, right. Like you scare me. A business executive."

"Hey, I can still take you with one hand tied behind my back."

"Oh yeah? Put your money where your mouth is." Steve shoved his plate aside and bent his elbow on the table, ready to arm wrestle his oldest brother like they had as kids.

Striker placed two twenty-dollar bills on the table and the match was on. Unfortunately two seconds later their intense concentration was interrupted by the unexpected arrival of Patrick.

"Did you talk to her?" Patrick's booming voice distracted Steve just long enough for Striker to pin his arm to the table.

"Gotcha!"

"Did I interrupt something?" Patrick belatedly asked.

"I was just teaching my baby brother a lesson," Striker noted, before stealing several of the French fries off Steve's plate.

"You're Steve's brother?" Patrick's bushy white eyebrows rose.

"Affirmative," Striker replied. "And you are?"

"He's the owner of this place and the pizzeria next door. He's also interested in our grandmother," Steve replied on Patrick's behalf. To Patrick, he said, "Yes, I did talk to my grandmother."

"And?" Patrick demanded.

"And my grandmother still appears to hold a grudge against you for that judging thing."

Patrick's face fell. "That was months ago."

"Understood. But it involved her *kolachkis*. She's very sensitive about her baked goods."

"Time out here," Striker ordered. He turned to face Patrick. "You're interested in our grandmother? In what way?"

Patrick rolled his eyes before pinning his gaze on Striker. "I already had this conversation with your brother."

Striker turned to Steve, who took great pleasure in knowing more than his brother.

"You're not gonna tell me, are you?" Striker said.

"You've got that right."

"Not a problem. I can read between the lines. Go on," Striker invited Steve and Patrick. "Proceed as if I weren't even here. I won't say a word."

"What can I do to make it up to her?" Patrick demanded.

Steve shrugged. "I have no idea."

"She's your grandmother. You should know what I can do."

"I'm not used to playing matchmaker for her. Usually she's the one doing that with the rest of the family."

"She's got a good heart. I know she's involved with a lot of things at our church."

"You both attend the same church?"

Patrick nodded.

"Well, that's a start."

"Not really. We've been going to the same church for years."

"Why didn't you ask her out before this?"

"She was still grieving for her husband."

Steve nodded. "She loved Granddad a lot. They were married for fifty years."

"My wife passed away ten years ago. We were only married forty years."

"I can't imagine what that must be like," Steve noted.

Patrick shook his head sadly. "So many marriages break up these days."

"Half of them. The rate is even higher in the Marine Corps, I think."

"But your parents have a good marriage."

"Yeah, they do."

"And your dad was in the Marines for many years, right?"

"Right."

"So you should know firsthand that it can work out."

"How do you know so much about my parents?"

"Like I said, Wanda and I go to the same church. The grapevine is very good."

"That's an understatement," Steve noted dryly. "I've seen intel that wasn't as efficient."

"You were speaking of marriage earlier, does that mean you are thinking of marriage and Chloe?"

"Whoa!" Steve held out his hands as if to prevent the older man from continuing down that road of discussion. "We haven't even known each other that long."

Patrick shrugged. "That doesn't matter. I knew my wife was the one the first moment I laid eyes on her. A month later, we were married."

"I don't believe in that love-at-first-sight stuff," Steve scoffed. "Besides, the first time I laid eyes on Chloe I knew she was a librarian. That's about it."

Patrick frowned. "What do you mean?"

"She'd deliberately worn this frumpy outfit. She claimed it was for some program they were doing at the library—where she dressed up as a dowdy secretary. But I think she was trying to fade into the background. It worked." Steve had no idea why he was telling Patrick this. Since Steve had only had half a bottle of beer, he couldn't blame his loose tongue on alcohol.

"Did it?" The question came from Striker. Steve had almost forgotten his brother was still with them, eavesdropping on their conversation.

"What do you mean?" Steve demanded, still irritated with his brother for beating him at arm wrestling.

"Just that you seem to be spending a lot of time with someone you thought faded into the background."

Steve shrugged. "I don't know. From the get-go, there was just something about her…."

"Ah." Patrick nodded. "Now that's more like it."

"What?" Steve demanded.

"*Just something about her.* That's how it was with my Irene. We just clicked."

It wasn't the first time Steve had heard about something just clicking. There was a history of that in his own family. His grandmother had just looked at his grandfather right after World War II and bingo. Love at first sight. And then there were his parents. His dad had seen his mom at a dance and that had been that. One look, that's all it took. Wasn't that how some song went?

But times were different now. Women were different. Relationships were different.

Besides, falling in love at first sight wasn't something you inherited in your genes.

Steve had thought he was in love with Gina and look how well *that* had worked out. He wasn't about to have his heart drop-kicked that way again.

What, one bad call and you're out of the game?

No, I just play it differently now. No strings. No attachments.

Yeah, right. So why are you having so much fun with Chloe?

Fun. He was having fun. Not falling for her.

Besides, she got it. She got *him.* She understood what was going on here.

Then she's smarter than you are, jarhead, his inner voice mocked.

Steve decided that talking to oneself was not very productive so he returned his attention to Patrick. "Sorry I couldn't do more to help you out."

Patrick shrugged. "I'm not giving up. I have an idea."

"Those four words have gotten plenty of men in trouble. Especially when there's a woman concerned," Striker said.

"Wanda is a very attractive woman."

Striker made a face and held up a hand. "Please. I don't want to go there. She's my grandmother."

"She wears that T-shirt that says Age Is Mind Over Matter, If You Don't Mind, It Doesn't Matter. I like that philosophy."

Steve just rolled his eyes. So did Striker.

"She's a passionate woman," Patrick continued. "She has a real passion for life, for everything."

Steve finished the rest of his beer in one gulp. Striker followed suit.

"You young people." Patrick shook his head. "You think you have all the time in the world. It ain't true. When you reach my age, you know better."

Steve knew one thing that was true. When he thought of a passionate woman, he thought of Chloe. Not his grandmother.

The minute Patrick left them alone, Steve said to Striker, "Now you know what I've been dealing with."

"Yeah. I don't envy you one bit. By the way, I didn't fall in love with Kate at first sight, you know."

Striker had married the Texas attorney several years ago and they now had a young son named Sean.

"So you didn't fall for Kate at first sight. Am I supposed to be relieved at that news or what?"

"No, you're supposed to pay attention. Because while I didn't fall for her at first sight, there was something about her…." Striker's expression softened before the mockery returned as he smiled at Steve. "So you'd better beware, baby brother. Sounds like you may be checking your heart out to this librarian."

"What's that stupid phrase you made up? Oh yeah, I remember now. That skunk just ain't gonna mate," Steve drawled.

"Deny it all you want. I know the signs. The skunk doesn't have to mate, but you and the librarian will. And here I was thinking you'd sworn off romantic entanglements after that last gold digger."

"Who says I'm romantically involved?"

"Rad."

"Like he'd know."

"He fell for a bookworm himself. He claims you're showing all the signs."

"He hasn't seen me, he's only talked to me on the phone."

"Okay, then you *sound* like you've got the signs. He's good at reading people."

"I'm glad to hear he's good at something."

Striker returned Steve's grin.

"Okay." Striker held up his hands. "Far be it for me to give you advice."

"Yeah, right," Steve scoffed.

"Let's return to more important matters." Striker placed his elbow on the table in preparation for another arm-wrestling match. "What do say about two out of three?"

"You're on!"

"I can't believe I let you talk me into this." Chloe shook her head as she fastened the Rollerblades onto her feet Saturday morning.

She'd had her hair cut during the week into a layered style that framed her face at the front while remaining at shoulder length toward the back. The up-to-date look gave her confidence.

It was one of those unexpectedly perfect Indian summer days that had everyone out in the park to enjoy what might be the last remnants of warm weather. Steve looked great in running shorts and a USMC T-shirt. He was obviously in excellent condition. She was seeing more of his muscular body than she ever had before. And she found she was totally enjoying the view.

She'd had to work a split shift on Thursday night so they hadn't gotten together then. But on Friday he'd brought her favorite Chinese takeout and they'd spent the evening watching Sweetie cavort around the living room.

Chloe had had to kitten-proof the place. Or try to. Sweetie still had a way of getting into things. Wherever there was a pile of books, the kitten would launch off them, making them slide onto the floor. And earlier this morning Sweetie had somehow managed to climb onto the top shelf of the built-in bookcases in the living room and then been too scared to jump back down.

Chloe had rescued her, not that Sweetie had been that appreciative. Instead she'd torn off to some new kitten adventure.

No, Chloe's life was no longer as neat and orderly as it had been just a short while earlier.

And for that, Chloe was truly grateful. She'd had no idea how staid she'd become. The old Chloe would never have agreed to go in-line skating.

Actually the new Chloe was having a few second thoughts as well.

"Hey, you're the one who said you'd always wanted to try in-line skating," Steve reminded her.

To which Chloe retorted, "I've always wanted to try hot-air ballooning too, but…"

"Great. We'll do that next weekend."

"Only if I survive this adventure first."

"Oh ye of little faith. Come on, stand up."

"Easy for you to say," she muttered.

"Here, hang onto me." Steve offered her his hand.

She stood, grabbing for his shoulders as her feet went in opposite directions.

"I've got you." He held her in one arm, her body pressed close against his. His deep voice rumbled against her. The thin cotton of her T-shirt and his provided little protection as her breasts pushed against his chest. "You're okay."

She wasn't so sure about that. Was it okay to have her heart hammering like a wild thing? Was it okay to go weak at the knees because of him? Her face rested against the warm cotton of his soft T-shirt.

He smelled good. Clean. Male. No cloying aftershave. He didn't need any to be sexy.

His hand moved up and down her back to reassure

her. She'd released his hand when she'd first started to feel herself falling and had grabbed his shoulders instead. Her head fit just under his chin. How nice just to stay here like this.

The renegade thought made her nervous.

And just like those turtles Wanda was so fond of, when Chloe got nervous she withdrew. A little. She'd made some giant strides, but there were still times when she had to pause and reassess things.

Since she still felt unsteady on the Rollerblades, she wasn't about to let go of Steve entirely, however. "Sorry about latching onto you that way." She belatedly shoved her glasses back into place.

"Hey, I don't mind, believe me." He now had his hands braced on her waist.

"I don't usually lose my balance like that."

"I have that effect on women."

She laughed. "So I've heard."

"Time to put your helmet on." He plunked it on her head.

It made her feel dorky looking but it wasn't as large as the helmet she'd worn on the Harley.

"Are you ready to try again?"

She was. He made her want to try all kinds of things again. Things she shouldn't even be thinking about. Things she'd never thought about before. Things she'd given up on. Things she'd never even attempted.

"You can do this," Steve told her.

Of course she could. She'd ridden on a Harley. She'd eaten sushi. She'd met his parents. What were a mere pair of Rollerblades compared to those things?

Confidence was an amazing thing. Once you got it, there was no telling how far you could go.

Chloe got as far as five feet down the path before realizing she was actually in-line skating. On her own!

Well, she was holding Steve's hand, but that was for moral support, not to prevent her from falling on her face.

"You're doing great," he congratulated her.

"I think the reason I felt so uncomfortable is that it doesn't feel like I'm on solid ground. It felt like I could go any which way."

Steve gave her a look. "Are you thinking again? Analyzing things?"

"No. I was just making conversation."

"*It's a nice day* is making conversation. You were definitely analyzing, which is intense thinking."

"It is?"

"Affirmative."

"Listen, it occurs to me that you're not being logical. On the one hand you accuse women of being too sensitive and emotional yet on the other hand you don't want me thinking too much. What, you just want me to stand beside you and gaze up at you adoringly?"

"If you were doing that in a wet T-shirt, it would be even better." His smile was pure male.

"So you're saying that all you're really interested in is a woman's breasts?"

"Of course not."

"Good."

"Great legs are also a good thing."

"Of all the chauvinistic…!"

His wicked grin made her pause.

Chloe sighed. "You were pushing my buttons again."

"You make it entirely too easy."

"Yes, I do. I'm going to have to work on pushing your buttons."

"I'm telling you, a wet T-shirt would do it."

"I didn't mean *those* buttons."

"You're so cute when you're serious."

"So you take pleasure in telling me."

He took pleasure in the feel of her fingers curved around his, in spending time with her, in watching her emotions flash across her face, in the way she wrinkled her nose before pushing her glasses into place to bestow a reprimanding look upon him. He got a kick out of her enthusiasm in trying new things and he couldn't resist the urge to tease her.

"How about some fennel cakes?" She pointed to a stand ahead. "My treat."

Five minutes later they were sitting on a bench near a fountain that was shooting water in the air in an aquatic ballet. Little kids sat around the edge of the fountain, totally wrapped up in the alternating rhythms of the display—leaping drops, darting spurts and liquid streams.

"Neat, huh?" She turned to face him.

"Yeah. Neat." But he wasn't referring to the fountain. Or the fennel cake. He was referring to Chloe. The librarian who had powdered sugar on her lush lips that he wanted to kiss. Again. And again.

So you'd better beware, baby brother. Sounds like you may be checking your heart out to this librarian.

Striker's warning echoed inside Steve's head.

"So how are things going with you and the bookworm?"

"Fine. How are things going with you and your bookworm?" Steve retorted.

"Outstanding."

"Then why are you bothering me? You don't need to borrow money or anything do you?"

"Very funny. Pardon me while I choke with laughter." Rad made several grunting noises.

"I hear indigestion comes with old age," Steve said. "You might want to see a medic about that."

"You're in rare form today."

"Yeah, I am, aren't I?"

"And so modest about it, too."

"Right. After all, all of us Kozlowski brothers are known for our modesty."

"And here I was thinking we were known for our sex appeal."

"Well, *I* am, but you're an old married guy with indigestion. No appeal there."

"Hey, I didn't call you to get hassled," Rad retorted. "I could have talked to Striker for that. He's better at it than you are."

"He's a legend in his own mind."

"Hey, I heard that," Striker said.

"Oh, didn't I tell you that Striker was in town visiting us?" Rad inquired with mocking innocence. "He's on the other phone line."

Steve was unfazed. "Listen, I just saw Striker in person a few days ago so he already knows how I feel about him."

"Bitter because I beat you at arm wrestling," Striker stated. "Yet you still think I'm a legend in my own mind?"

"You can't help it," Steve replied. "It comes from living in Texas now."

"You haven't been talking to Dad have you?" Striker's voice had turned serious.

"Of course I have."

"So he's still p.o.ed about me taking over King Oil? I thought he'd gotten beyond that."

"We didn't talk about you. Contrary to your belief, the world does not revolve around you. And it certainly doesn't revolve around Rad."

"I'm still on the line here," Rad growled.

"Yeah I know." Steve grinned. "Makes it even better to push two brothers' buttons at once."

"Striker, tell me again why we called this idiot?" Rad demanded.

"To harass him about the bookworm who's got him wrapped around her finger."

"She's a librarian. And she doesn't have me wrapped around anything. What's with you two? Don't you have more important things to jabber about? You sound more like matchmakers than Busha does. Is that what being married does? Turn your brain to mush and make you all sappy? What's it gonna take to convince you two that I'm not interested in marriage? I'm just here on leave for a few weeks, no big deal."

"It wasn't, until you hooked up with a bookworm," Rad stated.

"Rad, did you warn Steve about bookworms?" Striker asked.

"Affirmative," Rad replied. "The minute Steve told me about her."

"Hey, if you don't want advice then don't come crying to us about your love life when it goes bad," Striker told Steve.

"Roger that," Rad agreed.

"I've got a plan."

"Oh no," both his brothers groaned.

"Yes, but my plan is going to work, unlike your lame-brain plans."

"Famous last words," Rad said right before Steve hung up on him.

Despite what his brothers thought, Steve had things under control. He was an officer in the United States Marine Corps. He was trained to maintain control and successfully complete missions. And that's what he'd do with Chloe.

Romance was not an option. Not for either one of them. They were a team. Alpha Libras. Not a couple.

Steve wasn't in the best of moods the following Saturday. All week he'd told himself that everything was going according to his plans. Then he'd fall asleep and dream of Chloe at night. Wearing her sexy Chicago Bears nightshirt. Or wearing nothing at all.

That wasn't part of the game plan. So okay, he was experiencing a minor speed bump here. Nothing major. Nothing he couldn't handle. That didn't mean his but-tinsky brothers were right about him falling for Chloe.

The roar of a Harley interrupted his irritated thoughts. It wasn't his Harley. It was Patrick's Harley. The older man pulled to a stop by the curb in front of Wanda's bungalow.

"What are you doing?" Steve demanded.

"I told you I had a plan."

"That was more than a week ago."

"Well I had to perfect it now, didn't I?" Patrick retorted.

"Where did you get the Harley?"

"It belongs to one of my sons."

"The Chicago policeman?"

Patrick nodded.

That explained the machine, but it didn't explain Patrick's presence.

"And your plan involves you riding a Harley?"

Patrick nodded.

Steve suddenly didn't have a good feeling about this. But before he could comment, his grandmother came out of Chloe's house and joined them. Chloe was right by her side. Wanda had gone over to bring Sweetie a new toy, as she did every few days.

"What's going on here?" Wanda demanded.

"I thought you might like to go for a ride," Patrick said.

"No way!" Steve said before his grandmother could speak. "She's much too old to ride on a Harley."

There was a moment of stunned silence.

Then Chloe said, "Uh-oh." And shook her head.

"What?" Steve demanded.

Chloe sighed. "You've done it now."

"Done what?" he said.

"Too old, huh?" Wanda came right up to him, all four feet eleven inches of her, and poked her finger in the middle of his chest with such force that he winced.

"I just meant that—"

Wanda cut him off with a wave of her hand. "Not another word. I do not need you telling me how to live my life."

Steve almost said, "Why not, you tell me how to live my life all the time," but a warning look from Chloe told him to stay silent.

"I will do as I please." Wanda jabbed his chest again. "I have earned the right."

"Fine. I was just concerned about your safety. The back of a motorcycle is no place for my grandmother."

Wanda narrowed her eyes at him before marching right over to Patrick. "How do I get on this contraption?"

"Busha!"

Chloe took hold of Steve's arm to prevent him from marching after his grandmother. "You're just making things worse."

Steve did notice how surprisingly quick and agile Wanda was at following Patrick's directions and mounting the Harley, but that didn't make him feel any better.

Taking pity on him, Patrick told Steve, "We're just going to the pancake house down the street a few blocks."

"Then why don't you both walk there instead?" Steve demanded.

"We left our walkers at home," Wanda retorted. "Come on, Patrick. Step on it. Let's blow this pop stand!"

Chapter Nine

"**I** can't believe she did that." Steve stood in the street, staring at the quickly retreating back of his grandmother aboard Patrick's borrowed Harley.

"You dared her into it," Chloe retorted.

"Me? I'm the one who told her not to go!"

"No, you're the one who told her she was too *old* to go. *Big* difference."

"Well, she *is* too old."

"Apparently she's not. She seemed pretty spry to me as she hopped onto that Harley."

Steve turned to her, his exasperation apparent. "You were supposed to be helping me talk her out of it, not just standing there."

"Far be it from me to try and change your grandmother's mind once she's had it made up. You're the one who told me that she could be stubborn that way."

"Yeah, but she's never gone off the deep end like this before."

"Well, she's probably never had one of her grandsons tell her she's too old to do something before."

"She should have listened to me."

"Of course." Chloe nodded solemnly. "You're a Marine. Everyone should listen to you, right?"

"At least in the Marine Corps everyone follows a certain code of behavior."

"Unlike us rowdy civilians, you mean?"

Steve was a proud officer in the nation's oldest and proudest branch of all the armed services. You didn't join the Marine Corps because it was easy. Yet here he was, unable to get his own grandmother to obey his simple request.

Was this leave making him soft? His leadership skills had never been called into question before. But now Steve could feel this situation slipping out of his control and he didn't like it.

Time to call in reinforcements.

"Now what are you doing?" Chloe asked him.

"Calling my dad to tell him what his mother has done."

She looked at him skeptically. "Do you really think that's the right thing to do? Wanda certainly won't appreciate it."

"She butts into my life, I don't see why I can't butt into hers."

"Is that what this is all about? Payback?"

"No, it's about me being concerned about her." Steve turned away to concentrate on the phone call. "Dad, it's Steve. Your mother has gone off the deep end. She's just taken off on the back of a Harley with that guy who refused to give her the blue ribbon for her *kolachkis*. Remember, we talked about him when you came for dinner? Yeah, that's right." Steve nodded. "His name is Patrick. They went to the local pancake house….What do you mean, that doesn't sound too bad? She was on the back of a motorcycle.... I *did* try to stop her, she wouldn't listen to me. So what are you going to do about it? Nothing?... You've never been able to control what she does? Yeah, but she's older now.... Yeah, I told her that.... What do you mean uh-oh?... Okay, okay, so it might not have been the most politically correct thing to say...." Steve paused to listen to whatever his dad had to say. "Okay, fine. If you don't think there's anything to be worried about, it's your call. I just hope you're right." He disconnected the call.

By now, Steve was aggravated enough to chomp boulders. Which wasn't like him. While his brothers tended to get all riled up, he was the one who kept his head. The even-Steven one in the family, fair-minded and even-tempered. Sure, he might be adventurous, but that didn't mean he was a hothead.

So why was he getting so angry about this situation?

And why was he suddenly analyzing himself so much? He was a guy. He wasn't into studying his emotions like this.

Maybe he'd been hanging out with females too much lately by living at his grandmother's house. Which returned to his earlier concern that he was getting soft. Not physically. He began his day with fifty one-armed push-ups. But this emotional stuff...

Well, he'd be back on duty soon. Things would be back to normal then. He could always depend on the Marine Corps to keep the same reliable rock-solid values.

"So your father was okay with Wanda going off with Patrick?" Chloe asked him.

"He said there was nothing he could do at this point. That doesn't sound like my dad. He's always been a man

of action. Maybe being retired has made him soft."
There was that phrase again. "Driving around in an RV
like a tourist."

"He didn't appear to be soft to me when I met him."

"You don't know what he was like before," Steve
retorted.

"Wasn't he gone a lot before? On deployments?"

"Affirmative."

"You're so cute when you're serious." Chloe couldn't
resist teasing Steve.

"Very funny."

"What do you want to do now?"

Looking at Chloe, standing beside him in her jeans
and Radical Librarian sweatshirt, made him suddenly
want to yank her into his arms and kiss her until neither
one of them could think straight. He wanted to sweep
her up into his arms and take her into her house and
make love to her, touching every inch of her body, revealing all her secrets, discovering what made her moan
with pleasure.

She touched his arm. "Steve?"

He blinked. "Yeah?"

"Did you want to cancel our plans to go to Galena
for the day? We can wait until Wanda gets back if you'd
rather."

"I have no idea how long she'll be gone."

"I don't mind waiting."

Steve shook his head, as much to get those earlier
erotic images of him and Chloe out of his mind as to indicate that he didn't want to hang around here. "I'm not
her keeper, as my father pointed out. Although she could
certainly use one."

"I think it's sweet that you're so concerned about her."

Steve grimaced. "Sweet?"

"That's a good thing. You said your Harley was sweet."

"But not *nice* sweet. You meant nice sweet." Now he was really disgruntled.

"Sorry. Not the right image for a tough Marine like you, hmmm?"

"You've got that right."

"How about I think it's honorable of you to be concerned about Wanda?"

"That sounds better."

Steve's irritation was improved by the sound of the Harley's state-of-the-art machine as he revved the engine. Chloe climbed aboard with ease, slinging her sexy denim-clad leg over the motorcycle like a pro. How different from the mousy librarian who'd come to his grandmother's back door over two weeks ago.

He had yet to decide which was the real Chloe. There were so many sides to her. He got such a kick out of her willingness to try new things and her excitement at new experiences. She'd been a gung ho teammate, embracing his suggestions for new adventures with an open mind and a cute grin.

Even her glasses were cute, although they had kind of gotten in the way the last two times he'd kissed her.

Not that they'd slowed him down, however. Had he ever kissed a female who wore glasses? Yeah, but not since the tenth grade.

He felt Chloe cuddling closer. He wasn't sure if she knew she was cuddling. *Cuddling.* Another soft word. But he didn't know how else to describe what she was doing. Whatever it was, it felt good.

They headed west, past houses with pumpkins on the

porches and paper witches taped to the windows. Halloween was still three weeks away. By then he'd be back at Camp Pendleton in California.

Here the days were getting shorter and the weather played that roulette game—coming up summer like last weekend or cooler like today. But in California the days were pretty much the same. He never realized he missed the four seasons. Well, maybe not the snow so much.

They continued out of the city, heading across the state, past open farmland toward the Mississippi River and the town of Galena.

The open road had always given him a sense of peace that he'd never felt anyplace else. His twin brother Tom felt the same way.

Not that they were mind readers or anything. As kids they'd practiced playing poker, trying to read the hand the other one held. It hadn't worked worth diddly-squat.

Steve grinned at the memory.

He needed to e-mail Tom again. With his brother being posted in the Mid-East, they had to depend on occasional e-mails to keep in touch.

He wondered what Tom would think of Chloe. Like him, Tom had run into trouble with a female and his inheritance. Sure, Chloe knew about the money, but she also knew that this wasn't a romantic relationship.

So why did you want to grab her in your arms? an inner voice mocked him.

Doesn't sound real platonic to me.

No, his relationship with Chloe wasn't merely friendly. There was something else going on. There was definitely a male-female chemistry at work here.

Which was fine. They were both enjoying their time

together. No strings. No regrets. No commitments. Just having fun.

So why did his heart give a stupid jump when she snuggled closer against him?

"I think I've died and gone to heaven," Chloe murmured.

Steve sat across the table from her at one of Galena's best restaurants and stared at her in amazement. "Had I known that feeding you chocolate would have this effect on you, I'd have done it sooner."

"This isn't just any chocolate. This is the best. It's *orgasmic* chocolate."

Steve almost choked on his coffee.

Studying her face as she slipped another spoonful into her mouth confirmed her words.

There was something erotically sensual about the way she closed her lips around the spoon, the way she closed her eyes and inhaled deeply. Her throaty *mmmm* was making him hot. And making his jeans uncomfortably tight.

Steve shifted in his seat. Who knew that eating dessert could be such a turn-on? Or more specifically, that watching Chloe eat dessert could be such a turn-on.

Chloe's tongue darted out to lick a dab of chocolate from her full lower lip.

Why hadn't he noticed how sexy that bottom lip of hers was before? It required all his willpower not to lean over and nibble on that lip. That wickedly sexy lower lip.

What was wrong with him? Since when did he notice a woman's bottom lip? He'd never been into details like that before.

So what was it about this female that made him notice stuff like that?

"Mmmmmm." She slipped more chocolate into her mouth.

Ohhh, man. This was getting tough. He couldn't look away.

Was she deliberately trying to drive him crazy?

Steve frowned at the possibility. It was certainly something Gina would have done.

But Chloe wasn't like Gina, was she?

No way.

The vibration of his cell phone was a welcome diversion. A quick check of the caller ID told him that the call was from his grandmother. She still sounded irritated. "For your information, I got home just fine, so there was no need for you to worry."

"Thanks for reporting in."

"I don't report to you." She was getting all riled up again. "You'd do well to focus on your own life."

How could he do that when his focus remained fixated on Chloe and her orgasmic chocolate? Luckily Wanda hung up before he could say anything else that would set her off.

"That was my grandmother," Steve told Chloe. "She got home okay."

"I'm glad. Do you feel better now?"

Better? Now that Chloe had gotten him all wound up and ready to hit the sheets? Not really.

"I still think it's sweet...I mean honorable," she quickly corrected herself, "that you're worried about your grandmother. Especially given the fact that you're a lean, mean fighting machine, right?"

"Affirmative."

"Sometimes it's hard for me to remember you're a Marine," she murmured.

He wasn't pleased by her words.

"I didn't mean that as an insult in any way. It's just that with you being on leave and all, I'm not seeing the Marine side of you."

"I left my dress-blues uniform back at Camp Pendleton."

"It's not just the uniform. And maybe I didn't say that right. There are things about you that indicate your military background."

"The haircut."

She nodded. "And the way you carry yourself. The erect posture, the presence you project. You're obviously a man accustomed to giving orders and having them obeyed. A man used to leading others. I noticed that about you right away. But I've also seen you relaxed, having fun."

"You don't think Marines relax or have fun?"

"It's not the first image that comes to mind."

"It would be if you met all my brothers."

"They all like to have fun?"

"Affirmative. Tommy is probably the most fun-loving. But he's also the youngest."

"I thought he was only two minutes younger than you are?"

"One minute, but that still makes him the youngest."

"And you never let him forget it, do you?"

Steve grinned. "Not for one second."

"It must be nice being part of a large and loving family like yours."

"It has its moments."

"I'm sure it does." And being with Steve had its moments as well. He'd done so much more than just take her out on adventures and show her how to have fun. He'd made her remember the girl she'd been before her parents' death.

Janis had drilled it into Chloe's head that she shouldn't take stupid risks like her parents had by getting into that private plane for a ride that had ended up killing them. She'd trained Chloe to be quiet and not make any waves.

When she'd struck out on her own, those negative nuggets had remained buried deep in Chloe's consciousness, still guiding her behavior. Until now. Until Steve.

There was no changing her past but what about her future? Did she want to have a large family, like Steve's, with five children? She and Brad hadn't talked much about children, except in the broadest of terms, something along the lines of, "Someday, when it's convenient."

Life wasn't convenient. And if you were waiting for it to become that way, you'd wait in vain. Something else Steve had taught her. And Sweetie, who never cared whether it was convenient or not, if it was two in the morning or not. If she was lonely and wanted petting, she let Chloe know. She made waves. And she got results.

Maybe Chloe needed to take a page out of her kitten's book. But for now, she'd just focus on enjoying her day and be grateful that Wanda had said she'd look in on Sweetie while Chloe was with Steve. At least Wanda had said that before she'd taken off on Patrick's Harley. Steve had said Wanda was back home now, and she was a very reliable person. If she said she'd look in on Sweetie, she would.

Steve was also reliable. As he'd told her earlier, he did seem to mean what he said. She was tempted to tell him how sweet that was, just for the pleasure of pushing his buttons the way he so often pushed hers. She'd never realized how much fun could be had from teasing someone.

After leaving the restaurant, they walked along Galena's Main Street, a charming historic-preservation area where the nineteenth-century brick buildings created a uniformity, making it feel as if they'd stepped back in time.

When Chloe paused to look at one of the shop windows, Steve said, "Did you want to go in?"

"Do you mind?"

"No. I'm not one of those guys who's afraid of a little shopping. It takes more than that to scare me."

"Great!"

He may have spoken too soon. They went from there to a bookstore to an antique store to a linen store. That last one got him thinking how Chloe would look in any of the various beds on display. One was all girlie with flowers and ruffles, while another was black-and-white minimal. Steve liked minimal, especially if it applied to Chloe's night wear.

"Pretty impressive, huh?"

Steve nodded, having just caught sight of a red negligee tossed across the black satin sheets on the bed.

"They say that a bedroom should be your sanctuary, the place where you can rest and be at peace."

He would neither rest nor be at peace if Chloe were wearing that negligee, on those black satin sheets. He had to look away before he made an idiot of himself.

And he had to say something. What had she just said? Something about a sanctuary? "A rack is just a place to grab some shut-eye."

"A rack?"

"Marine term for a bed."

"What about a sanctuary?"

"There are places I go when I need peace and quiet. They're all outside, not inside. The Pacific Ocean at sunset, the Rockies at dawn. There's even a small beach in Chicago along Lake Michigan that I've visited from time to time. You can look back on the city from there but it's far enough away that people don't hassle you, especially this time of year."

She noticed him looking down at his watch. "Is it time to go home?"

"Not yet. I've got another surprise planned."

"What is it?"

"You'll see."

They drove outside of town. It wasn't until Chloe saw the sign that she realized what was going on. Balloon Rides. "You're kidding, right?"

"You said you'd always wanted to go up in a hot-air balloon," Steve reminded her. "Not having second thoughts are you?"

"Me? No way. How about you?"

"I've flown in F-16s," he noted dryly. "I think I can manage a balloon."

"Are you insinuating that this is a sissy means of transportation?"

"Only if the balloon has dainty flowers all over it."

It didn't.

They were greeted by a stocky man in his forties. He had the sun-bleached hair and tanned face of someone who spent a lot of time outdoors. And he wore a lime-green T-shirt with black lettering listing a Leonardo da Vinci quote. "Once you have flown,

you will walk the earth with your eyes turned sky-
ward, for there you have been, and there you long to
return."

He greeted them both with a big smile and a hearty
handshake. "Welcome folks. I'm Al Greenville, your
pilot for our flight today. We have the paperwork all
ready for you, if you'll just look it over and sign it."

Chloe tried not to be concerned that she had to sign
a legal release form in case of injuries. *We do not rec-
ommend balloon flights for people who are pregnant,
have chronic back problems, or who are at risk for having brittle bones.*

Brittle bones? As in doing this might make you
break some?

Meanwhile Al was busy informing them of what was
happening.

"We're going to be inflating the balloon with cold air
using a gas-powered fan. Once the envelope is full of
air, we stand the balloon up by turning on the burner and
heating the air inside."

Telling herself not to be a wimp, Chloe signed her
name and turned in her form. Then she focused her attention on the rainbow colors of the balloon before noticing how small the basket that would be carrying them
seemed to be.

Al said, "We'll gently ascend and float between five
hundred and one thousand feet wherever the wind takes
us. We'll be traveling above the treetops and below the
clouds."

Wherever the wind took them? What if it took them
someplace they didn't want to go?

Think positive, think positive, Chloe ordered herself.
This is something you've always wanted to do.

What if it ended badly like her parents' plane ride had?

Was she going to spend the rest of her life in fear? Being a turtle with its head stuck in and not moving forward? Or was she going to embrace adventures?

In no time, or so it seemed to her, they were in the basket and the time for doubts was done. They were up…aloft.

The blast of hot air into the balloon made her jump. Steve put a comforting arm around her. As time went on, she watched the farmland beneath them moving by. Rolling hills were dotted with golden accents, vibrant oranges and fiery reds.

"Cool weather is better for ballooning," Al told them. "We do a lot of flying in the summer, but the best flying is in the fall. It's a great way to see the foliage. The trees really are putting on a show this year aren't they?"

That show was nothing compared to the sunset they experienced a while later. The sky they were floating in became a changing canvas of colors, morphing from a hint of color to a flood of crimson light. Chloe was awed by the feeling of being totally immersed in the sunset.

She was still riding high when they descended for their landing. A sudden wind had picked up, but she didn't pay any attention to that until Al suddenly said, "Brace yourselves!"

Only then did Chloe turn her head to look and realize they were coming very close to high-tension power lines. Not a good thing, surely?

An empty field was coming up fast. No more time for fear or thought. Steve braced her against him, his body curved protectively around hers. Chloe bent her knees, as Al had instructed before takeoff, and hung onto the rope handle inside the balloon with one hand and Steve with the other.

They narrowly missed the electric lines before continuing their rapid descent, hitting the ground hard, the basket landing on its side.

Chloe landed on Steve. He cushioned her fall as the basket dragged along the ground before finally coming to a stop.

Her heart was pounding in her ears, adrenaline rushing through her system.

Okay, now she knew why people with brittle bones shouldn't do this. It was all perfectly clear to her.

What was also clear was the fact that her lower torso was pressed against Steve's, her legs entangled with his. She stared down into his eyes. Her glasses had fallen off in the crash landing, but she was close enough to see him clearly.

And that's when she knew. She wanted to be more than just Steve's teammate. She wanted to be the woman who made him feel like he was immersed in a sunset, the one he loved.

"Are you folks okay?" their pilot asked them.

"That was a little too close for comfort." Steve's voice was curt.

Chloe wondered if he was referring to their proximity to the electric wires or to their embrace. But there wasn't time to reflect on matters, as the ground crew gathered around them to secure the balloon and help them out.

There was plenty of time to think about things during the ride home in the dark, however. Steve had been unusually quiet after their landing. Chloe wished she knew what he was thinking. She didn't have a clue. She was having a hard enough time trying to decipher her own emotions.

She kept flashing back to that moment when she'd lain atop Steve, without the protective shield of her glasses, without any of her usual barriers in place, having just survived a scary experience. Looking into his eyes and knowing she wanted more.

There had been something in his gaze. Something she hadn't seen before. Gone were the usual glints of teasing humor. And in its place was…she wasn't sure. Desire?

What did it all mean?

She found out once Steve accompanied her into her house. She turned to switch on the lights in the foyer and instead found herself tugged into his arms. With one deft movement, he'd removed her glasses and covered her mouth with his.

There was no buildup as had occurred in their previous kisses. Instead there was a raw hunger that she welcomed. Because she felt that way herself, hungry for him. Hungry to prove they were both alive, that they'd survived, that he wanted her and she wanted him.

His hands slid beneath her sweatshirt, his fingers undoing the front fastening of her bra. His tongue tangled with hers, the thrust and parry making her moan with pleasure. That pleasure increased tenfold when he slipped his hand beneath her loosened bra to cup her bare breast in the palm of his hand, brushing his thumb against her nipple.

Exquisite sensations shot through her body, immersing her in the fires of passion until she was absolutely burning up. She broke off the kiss for the second it took her to peel off her sweatshirt. The moment she'd done that, Steve focused his attention on the buttons of her shirt, undoing them with quick efficiency and pulling her shirt open as if unlocking the doors to some priceless treasure.

Chloe returned the favor, shoving his leather bomber jacket off his broad shoulders and onto the floor. Her fingers fumbled with the buttons on his denim shirt because his mouth was consuming hers again and she couldn't see what she was doing. She was working from feel, and oh how good he felt. His skin was warm against her exploring fingers and she could feel his heart pounding as she ran her hands over his muscular pecs. Every ridge, every contour was a source of delight to her.

Coherent thought was totally gone, replaced by waves of a desire so powerful Chloe was unable to fight it. Why fight when making love was so much more pleasurable? All pretenses were erased, replaced with an edgy hunger made more intense with every caress, every lick, every nibble.

She felt wild and free, alive and aroused. This was no gentle gliding ride to the clouds, this was a rapid-fire jet-propelled takeoff straight to the stars. Passion throbbed deep within her body, calling out a need that only he could fulfill.

She rocked her hips against his, conveying the urges prowling her body. But instead of pulling her closer, Steve abruptly pulled away from her, leaving her feeling confused and bereft.

Chapter Ten

"I shouldn't have done that." Steve's voice was ragged. "I'm sorry. This wasn't a good idea."

Chloe didn't know what to say. Her lips retained the heat of his, her body still hummed where he'd touched her. Her mind was still cloudy with passion and couldn't quite compute what he was saying. She gathered her unbuttoned shirt together with shaking fingers.

His expression was unreadable. "I shouldn't have taken advantage."

"You didn't," she said. She fumbled to do up her buttons.

He handed her glasses to her. "It won't happen again."

"It wasn't your fault—"

He cut her hesitant words off with a brisk "Yes, it was. I should have known better. All I can do is apologize and assure you that it won't happen again."

"Why not?" How had those words slipped out of her mouth? An instant later, Chloe's face burned with a fiery blush as her brain caught up. He'd just told her kissing her was a bad idea. What did she need the guy to do, draw her a diagram?

"This wasn't part of our agreement." His statement sounded so matter-of-fact.

"Right." She took several steps away from him, wishing the floor would open up so she could disappear. Putting on her glasses made her feel only slightly less vulnerable. She could see that he'd refastened his shirt, showing none of her nervousness. He was totally impassive. A Marine with his war face on, fighting the clearly unwelcome emotional carrying-on of a female. "I'm sorry. You're absolutely right." He'd only signed up to be her buddy. Her Alpha Libras teammate. Nothing more. She was "the girl next door," the one he took on outings but did not take to bed.

The problem was that she was falling in love with him.

Humiliation saturated her soul. Her throat closed up and she felt her eyes burn with tears. There was no way she was going to cry. Do *not* cry, she fiercely ordered herself.

You're a big girl. Suck it up and try to get out of this situation without making more of a fool of yourself than you already have.

Refusing to look at him, she instead concentrated on smoothing a stray lock of hair behind her ear. She had to say something, make it appear that everything was okay even though it wasn't. But the words wouldn't come.

Steve had no such problem. "I mean it's not like either one of us is looking for any kind of romantic entanglement at this point, right?"

"Right."

"And even if we were, we're not right for that kind of thing. I'm a Marine. My time isn't my own. When duty calls, I have to go. You need someone who can be there for you 24/7."

Which made her think that Steve either believed she was a total wimp or he was just using it as an excuse to let her down gently. Had he been able to tell by the way she'd responded to him that she was falling for him? How could he not?

Did he really think she was some kind of needy, clingy woman? Was that why he was backing up as fast as he could?

He didn't seem surprised by the way she'd melted against him. Did this happen to him a lot? Women throwing themselves at him? Had he just been amusing himself at her expense, showing the staid librarian how to have fun, because she was so pitiful she didn't know how to do that on her own? Every one of those questions ate away at her.

But she refused to show it. Stick to the facts. She had her pride. No one had the right to imply she was a wimp. Not after the life she'd led. She might not have made waves, but she'd survived. "You make me sound like some kind of emotional wreck who needs a man as a crutch. I can assure you that nothing could be further from the truth. Not that I'm trying to convince you that we're meant for each other. I totally understand what you're saying." And meaning. That things were getting too close for comfort, so he was cutting his losses and heading out the door.

Another man finding her lacking. Just like Brad.

"We had fun together," she continued, her voice brittle. "But hey, it's time to move on. That's what you're trying to tell me, right?"

"In a manner of speaking."

"I have to give you credit for sticking it out as long as you did. Heaven knows, it must have been boring for you to get stuck hauling the staid bookworm librarian around, showing her how to have a good time."

"It wasn't boring."

"Well it certainly wasn't what you're accustomed to. Not your usual cup of tea, right?"

"That's true."

His words were like tiny daggers into her heart. "There you go then. And I'm terribly sorry if I embarrassed you by seeming to go all sappy on you for a moment there. Chalk it up to having just narrowly missed electrocution this evening."

Her words hit home for him, like a sucker punch to the gut, intensifying his guilt at having put her at risk. He was supposed to be showing Chloe how to have fun, not doing something that would endanger her. His reaction to that experience was still freaking him out.

Steve wasn't the kind of man who was afraid of much. Not that he hadn't ever experienced fear. He had. In combat situations. Not usually in emotional ones.

There were times to stand and fight and there were times to back off and regroup. And in this case, regrouping meant that it was time to hit the road and move on. He wasn't doing Chloe any good by sticking around.

He'd never meant to hurt her. That was the last thing he wanted to do. She deserved so much more than he could give her.

She gave him permission to leave. "I won't keep you any longer then. Thank you for spending so much time with me as you did."

Her ultra-politeness bothered him. "Don't make it

sound like you were some kind of charity case I was taking pity on."

"Why not? That's what it was."

"No, it wasn't."

"Then what was it? A project to keep you amused while you spent time home?"

"It wasn't like that either."

"Then what was it like?"

He couldn't answer.

His silence struck another blow to her heart. She wasn't sure how many more she could take. "You'd better go. The charade is over."

It seemed to her that he couldn't leave fast enough.

When the door closed behind him, Chloe made it as far as the comfy reading chair in the living room before curling up on it and angrily wiping away the silent tears.

It was okay, she'd be okay. She was home now, safe within her own four walls. She had her house. She had her books. She had friends. She even had a kitten now. She didn't need a man. No way, no how.

After leaving Chloe's house, Steve got on his Harley and just rode. He couldn't escape his own thoughts though. Or the memory of her sweet and sexy response. The feel of her breasts against his hands, the soft moans she made when he touched her there.

So much for being smart. Mission Alpha Libras had to be the stupidest idea he'd ever come up with. What had he been thinking? It was obvious to any idiot with half a brain that Chloe wasn't the kind of woman that you love and leave. He never should have kissed her once, let alone made out with her the way he had tonight.

That made it sound cheap, and there was nothing

cheap about Chloe. She was special. She needed some-one just as special. A man who'd always be there for her after her traumatic upbringing.

He couldn't get that look in her eyes out of his mind. She hadn't been wearing her glasses, so her blue eyes had looked incredibly beautiful and expressive. And they'd looked at him as if he were the one. The guy for her.

It was momentary insanity on her part. She hadn't re-ally fallen for him. She might think she felt something for him, but it was probably just a student falling for their teacher kind of thing. He'd taught her to be wild, it made sense that she'd be grateful for that. And pas-sion messed up your thinking.

She'd get over it. So would he.

But by the next afternoon he showed no immediate signs of recovery. He was eating another cheeseburger in Pat's Tavern, nursing another bottle of beer when Striker called on his cell phone.

"I forgot to ask you while I was up there in Chicago, but are you planning on stopping by Texas on your way back to California? For some reason, Kate has taken a shine to you and would love to see you. I can't imagine why."

"Maybe because I don't use dumb phrases like that skunk ain't gonna mate. And don't tell me I sound crankier than an armadillo in heat."

"I wouldn't dream of it." Striker wasn't very good at stifling his laughter. "So what went wrong with that librarian of yours that's making you crankier than an armadillo?"

"What makes you think this has anything to do with her?" His indignation reverberated around the room, making Patrick and several of the customers send him a look from behind the bar.

"Experience. So what happened?"

Steve lowered his voice. "I took her on a hot-air balloon ride and we almost got fried on electrical wires on the descent."

"Sounds exciting."

"Too exciting."

"Is that the problem? The librarian is too exciting for you?"

"No."

"So she's too dull?"

"She's too good."

"Good?"

"For me."

"And why's that?"

"She's had a tough life. Her parents died when she was a kid and she was shipped off to a relative who didn't want her. She needs some stability. A guy who can be there for her 24/7."

"And that's something a Marine can't promise."

"Affirmative."

"So why did you get involved with her in the first place?"

"I was just going to show her how to have some fun, to live it up a little, have some adventures."

"Like being electrocuted?"

"That wasn't part of the plan."

"Rad was right you know, as much as I hate to admit it. The best-laid plans go up in smoke when the right woman is involved."

"She's not right for me and there's no way I'm right for her."

"No? It sounds like in teaching her to walk on the wild side, you fell for her big time."

"If that's what it sounds like to you, then you need to have your hearing checked. I understand that's a problem as you get older."

"I can still take you in an arm-wrestling contest any day of the week, bro."

"I doubt that. You're domesticated now."

"You always try to push my buttons when you're on the defensive."

"Time to change the subject," Steve ordered. "Have you gotten any e-mails from Tom lately?"

"I got one yesterday. Why?"

"No reason."

"He's in the middle of a combat zone and he sounded calmer than you do."

"I'm hanging up now," Steve growled.

"Wait. What about you coming down here?"

"I'll think about it." But all he could think about after ending his call was Striker's accusation.

What did it really matter in the end whether Steve had developed feelings for Chloe or not? He wasn't right for her. They came from different backgrounds and were going different places. He was a Marine who could be shipped off to any hot spot in the world where he was needed. She was an intellectual librarian who loved books and her home. She listened to Mozart, he listened to Aerosmith. He didn't belong in her world and she didn't belong in his.

"You look like you could use a friend," Patrick noted before joining him.

"I'm not in the mood for polite conversation at the moment."

"I gathered that much from the way you were talking to whoever was on the phone."

"My brother Striker."

"Ah, is that what this is about? You two had an argument?"

"Not really."

"Are you still upset about me taking off with Wanda yesterday?"

Had it only been yesterday? Steve couldn't believe how much had changed since then. "I'm done giving my grandmother advice," Steve stated. "And I'm done acting as your go-between. If you have something to say to her, don't tell me about it."

"Fine by me." Patrick shoved a beefy hand through his thick white hair. "I won't be needing your assistance any longer anyway. We had a grand time at the pancake house. Cleared some things up."

Great. His grandmother and Patrick were starting a relationship while Steve had just ended his with Chloe. Maybe it was time that he took a page out of his grandmother's book and blew this place. Chicago no longer held much appeal for him. Maybe he should swing by Texas on his way back to Camp Pendleton.

That would certainly be better than sitting here moping.

Wanda came knocking on Chloe's door Sunday evening. "I've got a new toy for Sweetie," she announced cheerfully before falling silent at the sight of Chloe's red-rimmed eyes.

"It's allergies," Chloe hastily stated, tossing a crumpled facial tissue into the trash.

"You're not allergic to Sweetie, are you?"

"No." The kitten had been the one bright spot in her day.

"Are you allergic to stubborn Marines then?"

Chloe didn't know how to answer that.

"Did he do something stupid? He's my grandson and I love him, but that doesn't mean I don't think he can make mistakes." Wanda was wearing a T-shirt that said I'm Not Opinionated, I'm Just Always Right.

"I'm the one who made a mistake," Chloe replied.

"Whatever it is, we can fix it."

"No. Not in this case. I really don't want to talk about it, Wanda. I appreciate that you're just trying to help, but honestly…" Her throat tightened with emotion.

Wanda patted her hand. "I understand. But don't give up on my grandson just yet, okay? Things have a way of working out."

Wanda hightailed it out of Chloe's kitchen and into her own, where she almost knocked over her Texas turtle in her eagerness to reach for the cordless phone sitting on the kitchen table. "Young people," she muttered under her breath.

She'd known something was up but Steve hadn't said a word. And he'd taken off someplace without telling her where. Nursing his wounds, no doubt. Just like a man. Instead of talking about what was wrong.

"You need to speak to your son!" Wanda told her own offspring.

"Which one?"

"Steve, of course. You need to talk to him."

"About what?"

"About falling in love."

"What?"

"You heard me."

"I'm not butting into his love life and you shouldn't either." Stan sounded stern.

"That is no way to talk to your mother."

"I'm telling you this for your own good."

"No, you're not. You're saying it because you're afraid to talk to your own son about emotions."

"It's not something guys talk about."

"That is stupid."

"No, it's not. Not butting in is a good thing. If I were being nosy I'd want to know what was going on with that guy who picked you up on a Harley. But I'm minding my own business because you're a grown woman capable of making your own decisions. And because you won't listen to what anyone else has to say about it anyway. Neither will Steve."

"I am not making a big mistake. Steve is."

"Remember that Polish proverb you told me about?"

"Which one?" Wanda retorted. "I have told you about many over the years."

"Do not push the river, it will flow by itself."

"Yes, but in the wrong direction!"

"Maybe you should talk to Angela." A second later Stan had put his wife on the phone.

"What's wrong?" Angela sounded concerned.

"Your husband is afraid to talk to Steve about falling in love."

"Of course he is. That's no surprise. Men are bad enough at avoiding their emotions. Marines are even worse. Tell me what happened."

"Steve made Chloe cry."

"He wouldn't do something like that deliberately. He's not cruel. But I was afraid that things might get rocky."

"You could see this coming?"

"They haven't known each other that long...."

"They've known each other longer than Chuck and I knew one another before we got married."

"Times have changed."

"Not for the better."

"Maybe not."

"The Kozlowski men have a tradition of love at first sight. His brothers may not have been hit that way, but Steve was. I could tell."

"There did seem to be a lot of chemistry between them that night we had dinner together. But it's not something we can force," Angela said. "In the end, this really is between Steve and Chloe."

Wanda sighed. "I fear it may be the end of them both."

Early Monday morning Chloe busied herself in the reference section of the library, completing the daily routine before the library opened—setting up the desk, turning on the computers and copier machines, checking the book carts to see if more books needed to be added to the nonfiction display of recent releases. She walked by another book-display area featuring books on natural disasters, from the Johnstown Flood to the Chicago Fire.

Her personal life felt like a natural disaster. There had been no sign of Steve or his Harley at Wanda's house next door. She wondered it that meant he'd already headed back to California with its beaches full of gorgeous bikini-clad women.

She'd spent much of Sunday reliving what had happened to her—from the rough balloon landing, to Steve's passionate embrace, to his pushing her away.

A mistake. This was a mistake.

His words haunted her. So had the distant expression on his face. She'd never seen him like that before.

Not even Sweetie and her soothing purrs had been able to cheer up Chloe. Even the kitten had connections to Steve. But that didn't mean that Chloe was going to throw away the valuable lessons she'd learned during her time with Steve.

She'd changed over the past few weeks. She wasn't going to retreat back into her turtle shell again.

"Can you help me?" an older man inquired.

"Certainly." Chloe smiled encouragingly.

"I heard that a movie I liked, *October Sky,* out a few years ago, was based on a book."

As luck would have it, they'd recently done up a series of bookmarks with suggested reading materials on various subjects, one of which was "You Saw the Movie, Now Read the Book." Sure enough, Chloe found the book listed. "That would be *Rocket Boys* by Homer Hickam. It's in the biography section. Did you want me to show you where that is?"

The man nodded and smiled gratefully. "Thanks so much for your help."

Chloe had lunch with Lynn at their regular spot, Paco's Tacos, where she opened up to her friend, giving her a thumbnail version of what had happened. Chloe ended by saying, "I can't believe I was stupid enough to fall for a good-looking guy again. You'd think I'd have learned my lesson. But no. I'm dumb enough to get hit over the head with a stick a second time."

Lynn's face reflected her disappointment as well as her outrage. "I thought Marines were supposed to be heroic and honorable."

"It's not totally his fault. He made it clear that we were a team not a couple. Buddies. Nothing romantic. I'm the one who broke the rules." Chloe shoved her fork into her taco salad, moving the fresh ingredients around rather than eating them. "Why did I have to go and fall in love with him?"

"Maybe because he's an incredible hottie. And he took you on a hot-air balloon ride."

"And kissed me like he really meant it, like I was the reason he drew breath. Then he backs away and tells me it was all a mistake."

Lynn raised an eyebrow. "Sounds like the guy panicked."

"He's a Marine. They don't panic."

"Sure they do, if emotions are concerned. After all, he is a male and they all panic when they get cornered."

"I wasn't trying to corner him," Chloe said.

"I know you weren't. But just maybe the guy got cold feet."

"He told me that I needed someone who could be there for me 24/7. That, because of my personal history, I needed security."

"Well, he does have a point I suppose."

"He was just making excuses."

"If that's all he was doing, then why not just say that you didn't have anything in common or just say he'd call you and then not do it?"

"He was trying to be polite."

"Doesn't sound like it worked very well."

"And even if he was telling me the truth, that means he thinks I'm some kind of clingy, emotionally needy wimp."

"That's not how I'd describe you."

"I should hope not." Chloe speared a tomato with her fork.

"So what are you going to do now?"

"Go on. Forget him."

"Do you really think you can do that?"

"I'm a librarian. I can do anything."

Tuesday Chloe was scheduled to work the late shift, from one in the afternoon to nine at night. Since she had the morning off, she made an emergency run to the supermarket to get more kitten food. While driving home, she heard a Rod Stewart song on the radio, one they'd played the first day she'd met Steve when he'd driven her to the library.

She could still recall how he'd tapped out the beat to this song with his fingers against the steering wheel of Wanda's car. She'd watched his long fingers and wondered how it would feel to have him tapping out a sensual beat on her. Now she knew. It felt incredible. Better than she could ever have possibly imagined.

It was so difficult to believe that that night had only been a few weeks ago on a calendar, but ages ago experience-wise.

When Chloe saw Wanda hurry out of her house, she braced herself for more advice on how she should get back together with Steve. She wasn't prepared for the tears in the older woman's eyes and her expression of desperation. It was the face of a woman who'd just heard terrible news.

Chloe's heart stopped. "What's wrong? Did something happen? Is it Steve?"

Chapter Eleven

"Have you seen Steve?" Wanda demanded in a choked voice.

"No, I haven't. What's wrong? Has something happened?" Chloe repeated.

Wanda nodded, too upset for a moment to speak.

Chloe's entire body went cold. Terrible visions filled her head. Steve in a motorcycle accident. Him injured, sprawled out on the street, his blood on the pavement. "What happened?"

"Steve took off on that motorcycle of his." Wanda sounded as frantic as she looked. "He just roared out of here."

Oh no! Chloe could feel herself getting light-headed. She sank onto the front porch steps. The same steps where she'd sat with her knitting on her lap and admired

Steve as he fixed her car. The same steps where he'd handed a trembling kitten over to her.

"How bad is it?" Her voice was unsteady.

Wanda shook her head and wiped away tears. "It sounded very bad."

"He's still alive?"

"The last I heard, yes."

"What hospital is he in?"

"They're sending him to a military hospital in Germany."

Chloe blinked in confusion. "Steve was in an accident and they're sending him to Germany?"

"Steve was in an accident?" Wanda repeated, her forehead creased in obvious confusion.

"I thought that's what you said?"

"No."

"Then who is being sent to the hospital in Germany?"

"Steve's twin brother Tommy. He was seriously injured in an ambush in the Middle East. When Steve heard the news, he just took off. I thought maybe he went to see you at the library?"

"No."

"Where could he have gone? He was so upset, I hate to think of him all alone. He needs to be with his family at a time like this. His parents are coming over. They just phoned me with the news a few minutes ago."

Knowing how close the brothers were, Chloe could only imagine how upset Steve must be.

Where would he go at a time like this? She figured he'd want to be alone. Then it suddenly hit her. *Sanctuary.* She remembered him mentioning a special place of his downtown along Lake Michigan.

"I may know where he is. Let me check it out." She gave Wanda her cell-phone number. "If you hear anything, let me know."

Wanda hugged her. "Please, just find Steve and bring him home."

"I'll do my best," Chloe promised.

Steve needed to be alone until he got himself under control. The news of his twin's injury had come on the heels of his own discomfort that something was wrong. When he'd asked Striker yesterday if he'd heard from Tom, Steve hadn't really had any premonition of imminent danger. But in the middle of the night, Steve had woken in a cold sweat, grabbing his left thigh, just above the knee.

He'd tried to tell himself that it had been a nightmare, nothing more than that.

But it hadn't felt like any nightmare he'd ever had before. Unless you counted that time that Tom had had appendicitis and Steve had felt his pain in his dreams that night.

But that had been years ago, when they were kids. He'd started to wonder if he'd imagined the connection, if the story had grown in his head over the years. Now he knew better.

He also knew, without having to be told, that his twin was fighting for his life.

And so here Steve was, thousands of miles away, willing Tom to survive with a fierce intensity that was all-consuming.

He'd been sitting here for hours now.

Maybe he should have gone to a church and prayed. But this was his special sanctuary. One of them, anyway. He'd come without even thinking about it, just hopped on his Harley and headed straight here. To think.

Chloe stared at the isolated figure of a man sitting on top of a picnic table, his elbows resting on his denim-clad knees, his shoulders hunched forward. He was wearing the brown leather bomber jacket she'd come to know so well. But he had none of his customary confidence.

She looked around. They were alone. The chilly beach was deserted this time of year. The neighboring few park benches were empty, the grass covered with fallen leaves. A solitary beam of sunlight briefly bolted out of the otherwise cloudy sky.

Just a few weeks ago Chloe would have kept her distance, not wanting to intrude on someone else's space or privacy.

But now her one thought was that Steve was hurting, and she didn't want him to be alone. So she came closer, sliding up onto the table beside him without saying anything. Still without saying a word, she put her arm around him to let him know she was here for him.

"How did you find me?" His voice was ragged.

"I remembered you telling me that you had a special place. I checked all the beaches until I reached the right one. Wanda sent me to bring you home."

"Is there any more news?" Steve hadn't realized he'd left his cell phone back at his grandmother's house until he'd gotten down here. "I don't have my phone with me."

"No more news. I called Wanda a minute ago to tell her I'd found you."

"I felt it, you know." He turned his head to look at her, his green eyes bleak. "In the middle of the night. A red-hot pain in my leg. I knew something was wrong. With Tom. I told myself I was just dreaming it, but I knew. I'm a Marine. I know how quickly things can go wrong. You put it out of your mind, though."

She reassuringly rubbed her hand along his arm. She didn't know what to say to make him feel better.

"I've just been sitting here thinking, willing Tom to live, not to give up. But that's what I did. With you. I gave up without a fight."

Her hand stilled. "I don't understand."

"This situation with my brother is a sharp reminder that life isn't open-ended and that we shouldn't waste time. We should grab onto today, because there are no guarantees that there will be a tomorrow. Instead of being afraid of that, we need to embrace it, to embrace life." Steve reached out to trail his fingers down her cheek, his eyes intense with emotion. "I thought you needed someone to give you security and stability. But maybe what you need even more is someone who will love you for the rest of his days, however many days that may be. And maybe you'll decide that you *do* need more than that, but I'll never know for sure if I don't say anything." He reached for her hand, threading his fingers through hers. "I'm in love with you. There was just something about you that very first night I met you. My older brothers teased me about that, warning me that I was falling for you. But I was cocky and I assured them that I wasn't about to jump back into the romantic fire again. Not after Gina."

Steve paused a moment and looked down at their joined hands. "But I was just blowing smoke in their faces. They weren't buying it." His gaze returned to hers. "And each time I kissed you, I tried to tell myself that we were just teammates. That we were just having fun. But I knew that it was more than that. And when we almost hit those electrical wires...I snapped."

"You pushed me away."

He nodded. "Because I was being noble, because I was scared. Because I thought you deserved someone better than me. Because I thought we didn't have enough in common. But we have the most important thing. I love you and I think there's a good chance you may love me, too. You're the one for me, the one I want to marry and spend the rest of my life with."

Marry?! His proposal caught Chloe totally unprepared. She hadn't seen this coming at all.

She was afraid to believe it was true. She could tell how devastated he was by the news of his twin's injury. Stress made people do strange things, things they later regretted. She didn't want Steve saying anything he wished he hadn't later. "I know you're upset right now."

"Affirmative. But I'm also thinking more clearly than I have in a long time. What?" He questioned the doubt he must have seen on her face. "You still don't believe that I mean what I say and I say what I mean?"

"I believe you're got to be terribly concerned about your brother and that you're in the middle of a family crisis—"

The sound of Chloe's cell phone interrupted them. Chloe answered and then quickly handed the phone over to Steve. "It's your grandmother."

She could tell by his replies that Wanda needed him to return immediately.

"You need to be with your family now," she said the moment he disconnected the call.

Steve nodded his agreement. "Our conversation isn't over. We need to talk."

She nodded.

Steve drove behind her all the way home, as if looking after her. She wanted to tell him it wasn't necessary, but a part of her was touched by his chivalry even in the face of his own personal crisis. But that was Steve.

His grandmother and his parents were all waiting in the drive when they pulled up.

Chloe would have left them alone but Steve took hold of her hand as she got out of her car and didn't let go. The words flowed around her, details about a charter flight Striker had arranged to depart from Midway Airport for Germany within the hour. Then they were leaving.

Steve stood apart from his family for a moment to be with her. This time she was the one who raised her hand to cup his cheek. "You go see your brother. I'll be waiting here when you get back and we'll talk then."

"Count on it," Steve said gruffly before kissing her with a passion that said so much.

It was only after Steve had gone that Chloe realized she hadn't told him she loved him.

"Another day, another dollar," Lynn noted with a grin as she met Chloe at the staff entrance to the library two days later. They were the first ones in this morning. "Have you heard from your Marine yet?" Lynn asked while moving through the library to turn on lights.

Chloe shook her head. "Not yet."

"How long has he been gone now?"

"Fifty-two hours and—" Chloe checked her watch "—forty minutes, but who's counting?"

"Right. You miss him. Did he leave a number where he could be reached?"

Chloe nodded. "Several of them, including his cell number. But I don't want to bother him. Not with all he's got to handle. I did get an e-mail from Wanda saying that Tom's condition was stable now, so that's a good thing."

Chloe had called Lynn the night Steve had left for Germany, and had told her what had happened. They'd spent over an hour on the phone.

"Have you thought about his proposal?" Lynn asked.

"I haven't thought about much else."

"And?"

"And I don't know. He may have changed his mind about things by now."

The arrival of Martin, the library branch manager prevented any further personal discussion. A staff meeting took up a good part of Chloe's morning.

She spent the next few hours on the reference desk, answering phone questions and patron requests. The latest one came from a beaming woman in her early fifties. "My daughter just got engaged and she wanted me to get some books on planning a big wedding. I was starting to think she'd never get married."

After checking the subject heading on her computer, Chloe led the excited woman over to the area where the books on weddings were shelved. "I had a big wedding and I just loved it. How about you?"

"I'm single."

"Well when you do get married, would you like a big wedding?"

Chloe hadn't really thought about it before. But now that she did, she realized that she didn't want a huge wedding. Quite the opposite in fact. Something small but meaningful. Maybe even adventurous. She smiled. That was the effect that Steve had on her. One of the effects anyway. To live her life more adventurously.

She loved him. She had no doubt of that. Even though they may not have known each other for a long period of time, she felt she'd always known him in some ways.

But she didn't know if he'd feel the same way when he returned from Germany. She certainly wasn't going to hold him to statements made during an incredibly stressful time for him.

Returning to the reference desk, Chloe concentrated on completing a departmental report on the computer. Out of the corner of her eye, she caught sight of someone standing in front of the desk.

"I'll be right with you," she said, her gaze remaining on the computer screen as she saved her file. "I was so involved I didn't realize…" Her voice trailed off as she turned to find Steve standing there, in his United States Marine dress-blues uniform. He was a very impressive and totally unexpected jaw-dropping sight.

Chloe was too stunned to speak for a second. Then she said, "Wha-at…what are you doing here? Are you okay?"

"I couldn't wait any longer."

She could scarcely put together complete sentences. "Your brother?"

"I saw him." A shadow passed over his face. "His leg

is in pretty bad shape, but at least he still has it. He'll need a lot of medical care, but his life is no longer in danger. Things could have been much worse. Anyway, he ordered me to get my butt back here."

"Why did he do that?"

"Because he's smart.

"He's really going to be okay?"

Steve nodded. "It may be rough going for some time, but we Kozlowskis are a tough bunch."

"Sure you are." She blinked away the threat of tears. "You're Marines."

"And you're a librarian. Which means you're good at answering questions."

She figured he wanted information on his brother's medical condition. Or something along those lines. She'd do whatever she could to help him. "If we don't know the answer, we know where to find it."

"I'm glad to hear that. Because I'm here to ask you a very important question."

"You are?"

He nodded solemnly before stepping over to the opening next to her desk. She moved her office chair a bit to give him more room.

Keeping his eyes on hers, Steve took hold of her hand and slowly went down on one knee. "Chloe Johnson, I love you and I want to spend the rest of my life with you. Will you marry me?" He opened the ring box he held in his other hand.

It was the first time Chloe had ever shrieked in a library in her entire life. It wasn't a loud shriek, but it was definitely a shriek.

She immediately pressed her trembling fingers to

her mouth as if to prevent further outbursts. The hand he held was shaking, but his hold was firm and solid.

Her eyes filled with tears. "Are you sure?"

Steve nodded. "I'm not only sure, I'm positive. Without any doubt whatsoever."

"Then yes, I love you, too! And yes, I'll marry you."

He stood and took her in his arms, lifting her and swinging her around, right off her feet. "When?" he demanded. "Now?"

"What?" As he set her back on the ground, she lifted her hands to adjust her glasses, which had slid down her nose. "What do you mean now?"

"Let's elope right now. The King Oil jet is standing by to take us to Las Vegas. Just say the word."

It was all happening so fast!

"Come on, Chloe. Take this leap of faith with me. You won't regret it," he promised her.

And here it was. Her turning point. She had the choice to play it safe and plan for a long engagement or to trust her heart and take the chance. To live an adventurous life. To take a risk. A leap of faith.

The old Chloe would never have dared such a thing. But the new Chloe realized with a sudden insight that while Steve was the catalyst for the recent changes in her life—the newfound confidence and renewed determination to live life—those changes came from *within Chloe*. They had been within her all the time. Steve had been the key to unlocking them, but they were *her* strengths.

That knowledge gave her courage.

But enough courage to elope?

Lynn appeared out of nowhere. She must have heard

what was going on because she said, "If you're worried about Sweetie, I'll kitten sit for you while you're gone."

"What do you want?" Steve asked Chloe.

Her voice shook as she admitted, "I want it all. The Marine, the kitten, the bungalow."

"You can have it all. You just have to believe."

And just like that, she knew. Her smile came slowly before turning into a full-blown grin as she tugged his head down to hers. "I do believe. And yes, I will elope with you."

Steve kissed her, then swept her up in his arms. Their audience, patrons and staff, applauded his romantic gesture and called out their good wishes as he carried her out of the library and out to his Harley.

Six hours later...

"I was told that this is the best wedding chapel in Las Vegas," Steve told Chloe as their limo came to a stop. They'd already visited one of the city's exclusive shops and gotten Chloe the gorgeous dress she was wearing. The white georgette strapless gown had a tea-length A-line skirt. The ankle-strap white shoes were also brand new, and the sequins along their edge made her feel rather sassy. Her bouquet of a dozen hand-tied blush roses was simple and elegant.

The car door opened, but it wasn't their uniformed limo driver who greeted them. Instead Striker poked his head inside. "What took you so long?" he asked with a grin.

"What are you doing here?" Steve demanded.

"You don't think we'd let you get married alone, do you?" Striker said. "No way."

"But we used the King Oil jet."

"Right. Did I fail to mention that we have more than one?"

"Yeah, you did."

They got out of the limo to find a small crowd waiting for them. Not only Striker, but his wife Kate and their small son, Sean. Rad was there along with his wife, bookseller Serena. And Wanda!

Chloe couldn't believe her eyes. "But I thought you were still in Germany."

"No, I flew back with Steve. Tom has his brother Ben and his parents with him. He didn't need me right now. Steve does." She hugged him and then Chloe. "I'm so pleased for the two of you. I told you that you'd like her," she added with a jab at Steve.

"How did you know we'd be at this wedding chapel?" Chloe asked.

"I was the one who did the research on the Internet for Steve about wedding chapels," Wanda confessed.

"Enough talking," Striker proclaimed. "Let's get this show on the road."

Steve pulled Chloe aside. "Are you sure you know what you're getting into here?"

"I'm not only sure, I'm positive. Without any doubt whatsoever." Chloe deliberately repeated his earlier words. "And I can't wait," she assured him before kissing him.

He framed her face with both hands. "Do you have any idea how much I love you?"

"I'm counting on you to show me as soon as we start our honeymoon."

"Count on it." He straightened her glasses for her. "But it may take me a few decades to really convince you how much I love you."

"Are you insinuating that I'm a slow learner?"

"Not at all." Steve grinned. "For a librarian, you catch on fast."

"Oh yeah?" She shot him a saucy smile. "Well, for a Marine you…"

"Yes?"

"…are a keeper."

* * * * *

Watch for Cathie Linz's MEN OF HONOR *series
to continue with Tom Kozlowski's story,*
LONE STAR MARINE,
*coming in February 2006
only from Silhouette Romance.*